P9-DCH-985

Lily Quench
and the Hand of Manuelo

NATALIE JANE PRIOR

Illustrations by Janine Dawson

PUFFIN BOOKS

Visit Lily's Web site at
www.lilyquench.com

PUFFIN BOOKS
Published by the Penguin Group
Penguin Young Readers Group, 345 Hudson Street, New York, New York 10014, U.S.A.
Penguin Group (Canada), 10 Alcorn Avenue, Toronto, Ontario, Canada M4V 3B2
(a division of Pearson Penguin Canada Inc.)
Penguin Books Ltd, 80 Strand, London WC2R 0RL, England
Penguin Ireland, 25 St Stephen's Green, Dublin 2, Ireland
(a division of Penguin Books Ltd)
Penguin Group (Australia), 250 Camberwell Road, Camberwell, Victoria 3124, Australia
(a division of Pearson Australia Group Pty Ltd)
Penguin Books India Pvt Ltd, 11 Community Centre, Panchsheel Park,
New Delhi—110 017, India
Penguin Group (NZ), Cnr Airborne and Rosedale Roads, Albany, Auckland,
New Zealand (a division of Pearson New Zealand Ltd)
Penguin Books (South Africa) (Pty) Ltd, 24 Sturdee Avenue, Rosebank, Johannesburg
2196, South Africa

Registered Offices: Penguin Books Ltd, 80 Strand, London WC2R 0RL, England

First published in Australia and New Zealand by Hodder Headline Australia Pty Limited,
member of the Hodder Headline Group, 2004
Published by Puffin Books, a division of Penguin Young Readers Group, 2004

1 3 5 7 9 10 8 6 4 2

LIBRARY OF CONGRESS CATALOGING-IN-PUBLICATION DATA

Prior, Natalie Jane, 1963–
Lily Quench and the hand of Manuelo / Natalie Jane Prior.
p. cm.
Summary: When Lily, Queen Dragon, and King Lionel follow Murdo in his flight to the Black Mountains, they become involved with a revolution led by the mysterious Manuelo.
ISBN 0-14-240222-2
[1. Revolutions—Fiction. 2. Dragons—fiction. 3. Fantasy.] I. Title.
PZ7.P9373Lke 2004 [Fic]—dc22 2003070756

Printed in the United States of America

For Amelia and Lewis

Some Old Friends...

Lily Quench

Last of the dragon-slaying Quenches of Ashby, Lily and her friend, Queen Dragon, drove the Black Count's army out of Ashby and restored the lost prince, Lionel, to his throne. Lily later rediscovered her family's secret weapon (metal-eating Quenching Drops), rebuilt Ashby's fortunes by discovering the Treasure of Mote Ely, and tracked down the location of the magical Eye Stones to prevent them being used in an invasion from the Black Empire.

Queen Dragon

Sinhault Fierdaze (known to her friends as Queen Dragon) is a three-thousand-year-old crimson dragon, the size of a four-story house. When not in Ashby, she lives in a volcano, where she keeps a stockpile of treasure to snack on when she's hungry (dragons eat metal).

King Lionel of Ashby

The son of King Alwyn the Last, who was killed at the Siege of Ashby during the Black Count's invasion.

Queen Evangeline of Ashby

Born Evangeline Bright, and a former supporter of the Black Count, Evangeline helped drive the count's forces from Ashby and later married the king.

Crystal Bright

Queen Evangeline's shifty mother, Crystal, used to work for the Black Count and still complains that things in Ashby have never been the same since the Black Squads left. She worked briefly as a spy for General Sark.

Mr. Hartley

The Minister of the Ashby Church, Mr. Hartley was driven out of Ashby as a young man by the Black Count's army. Mr. Hartley helped Lily restore the lost prince, Lionel, to the throne of Ashby.

Dr. Angela Hartley

A former slave of the Black Count, Angela was the foster mother of his son, Gordon, for many years. She was rescued and reunited with her husband and has returned to live and work in Ashby.

Murdo

Born two thousand years in the past, Murdo joined the army Gordon was training at the Castle of Mote

Ely, and was feared as a cruel bully. Murdo was pushed down a well by his brother during a quarrel and badly injured. He was brought forward into Lily's time so his life could be saved.

Gordon, the Black Count

The only son of the Black Count who invaded Ashby when Lily was a baby, Gordon lost his empire to the treachery of his father's friend, General Sark. He disappeared into the past through a magical Eye Stone in the Black Mountains.

Manuelo

A mysterious cloaked fighter from the Black Mountains, Manuelo tried to steal the Treasure of Mote Ely from the vaults of Ashby Castle. He was foiled by Queen Evangeline and escaped. Nobody knows his true identity.

King Dragon

Thousands of years ago, during the Great War of the Dragons at Dragon's Downfall in the Black Mountains, Queen Dragon's long-lost fiancé led a small party of dragons through an Eye Stone in search of help. He has never returned.

The Black Mountains & Mining Districts under General Sark

The Campsite & Eye Stone

Valley of Dragon's Downfall

Dragon's Neck Peak

Underground River

River

Valley of the Citadel

Valley of Mine II & Mine III

The Citadel

Mountain Pass

Road to Ashby

chapter one

Escape of the Prisoners

The piece of wire made a scraping noise as it wiggled in the lock. The fingers holding it were dirty and purple with cold around the ragged nails. There was a click, and the wire scraped again. Someone's teeth chattered in the darkness. Mine III in the Black Mountains was always cold, and the prison cells on the lower levels were coldest of all.

"Sssh!" said Toni. Her face was a pale pinched smudge in the enveloping gloom. "You're making too much noise. They'll hear!"

"I'm being as quiet as I can."

Patterson twitched the wire one last time. There was another click inside the lock, and this time the gate creaked softy open. The four prisoners, Sim, Toni, Patterson, and Wilcox, crept out into a narrow passage. Normally there were guards there on duty, but not long before they had all run away. A Black Squad soldier had summoned them, yelling that Manuelo was in the neighboring Mine II and that they had to stop the attack.

"Manuelo must be out here somewhere!" whispered Sim excitedly.

"Uh-huh," said Patterson. He did not sound very interested. "Which way do we go now?"

"Up those steps."

They crept up a short flight of stairs and passed several other cells. Prisoners were crying out in them, some from cold, others from the pure misery of their situations. Desperate hands reached out between the bars. "How did you get out? Free us, too! Let us go!" But the escapees had no time to stop. As they hurried past, the other prisoners wept and shouted and cursed. A tear ran silently down Toni's cheek and dropped off onto her coverall collar, where it froze.

On the next level they reached the guardroom with its stove—gone out, as if it had been forgotten—and wanted posters on the walls. The guards' supper was still on the table, and the prisoners fell on the cold cups of tea and rubbery sandwiches and devoured them. Then Patterson picked up a lantern that someone had left behind and looked at the posters. The biggest one showed a scowling boy in a posh uniform. Underneath the words "MOST WANTED" was the name "GORDON."

"That's the old Black Count's son," said Wilcox. "He's been missing for months. Now that General Sark's in charge, I bet he'd give his eyeteeth to catch him. Who's this?" he went on, pulling down a picture of a girl with long wavy hair and a silver helmet on her head. "Lily Quench, eh? Like the hat."

"Come on, you dope," said Patterson. He took the poster of Lily Quench and put it in his pocket with the last sandwich, which he had palmed off the plate. Toni grabbed a greatcoat from a hook in the wall. Now they were leaving the prison section and entering the tunnels of Mine III.

"This way." Toni took a few steps along an

adjacent corridor. Ahead they could hear distant shouts and grating noises, punctuated by sharp thuds as if people were throwing things. The tunnels of Mines II and III ran very close to each other, and a serious fight was obviously going on in the adjoining mine. Wilcox grabbed Toni's arm and held her back.

"No. We can't join Manuelo now. We have to escape."

"I want to help Manuelo!" Toni struggled, but Wilcox held on tightly. He grabbed her collar and shook her.

"Do you want to get killed? If we go down that tunnel, we'll run straight into Sark's Black Squads. We've got to go in the other direction. Then we can double back and join Manuelo's forces from the rear. Now, tell us the way out!"

"It's this way," said Sim apologetically. Toni hissed, and he shrugged. "He's right, Toni. We're no use to Manuelo if we're dead."

Wilcox pushed her, protesting, in the opposite direction. Patterson walked on ahead, shining his stolen lantern over the rough-cut floor.

"Manuelo!" shouted Toni. "Manuelo!"

Sim whispered something in Toni's ear, and she fell quiet. But despite their fears, there was nobody to hear them pass. The miners and their overseers, the Black Squads who guarded the mines, had all vanished from their posts. Mine carts half full of valuable ore had been abandoned in the tunnels, and in one corridor they found a jackhammer, still warm and smelling of gasoline.

Level by level, they climbed toward the surface. Finally they reached a narrow flight of steps, leading up at a steep angle to a metal concertina gate. Patterson wrenched it open, and the prisoners came out at last onto a rocky slope.

An icy wind hit them. It cut through their thin coveralls and smeared their clothes against their bodies. Sim yelled, but the words were ripped from his mouth. In any case, everyone knew what he was saying: a blizzard was coming. In the Black Mountains, with winter starting, there would be no chance of surviving without shelter.

"I told you this was the wrong way!" cried Toni. She clutched the stolen greatcoat tightly around her shoulders. "We've got to get back inside. We'll freeze in no time!"

"Wait a minute." Patterson strode forward through the whirling snow. His lantern light glanced off the ice crystals. "What's this?"

"It's a dragonet!" Sim ran after him. He stared in wonderment at the sleek black machine that stood parked in the lee of a rock. "Where's its crew?"

Patterson grinned. "How about here?"

"I'm not getting in that thing!" cried Wilcox.

"Nor me!" said Toni. "I want to find Manuelo!"

"No," said Sim. "He's right. Don't you see? This is our chance to tell the rest of the world what's happening in the Black Mountains. We can bring back help. We can drive the Black Squads out of the mines for good!"

"Whatever you like. All I know is that I'm getting out of this cold." Patterson snapped back the clip that held the cockpit lid in place, recoiling as his bare skin touched the metal. He clambered up three or four toeholds in the side of the dragonet and lowered himself into its cockpit. The others quickly followed. It was too cold to stay outside a moment longer.

By the time they had all squashed into the cockpit, there was barely room to close the lid.

In the pilot's seat, Patterson rubbed his hands together and started fiddling with the controls. There were a few dials, a central joystick, and two levers, one labeled UP, the other DOWN. Patterson punched a red button marked IGNITION. The control panel lit up, and the dragonet juddered violently.

Wilcox yelled and grabbed his seat, and Sim and Toni grabbed each other. A belch of black smoke billowed up around the machine. Two red lights came on at the front like eyes, and the whole dragonet vibrated like an angry bee.

"Hold on, baby," Patterson muttered. "Hold on." He reached for the UP lever and pulled it toward him. The dragonet lurched and lifted off the ground. Sim gasped and covered his eyes. Toni screamed, and Wilcox clung to the seat with all his might.

The dragonet rose above the valley floor. In its thin searchlights they saw scenes of destruction and desolation. Men in black uniforms swarmed like ants across the churned-up snow. The miners' flimsy barracks stood surrounded by a ring of tanks, motorbikes, and dragonets; one of them was burning, and captive miners were lying facedown in the snow. Then Mine III disappeared in a swirl of snowflakes, and there was nothing but the blizzard and the night sky stretching out before them.

They were free.

The dragonet flew on through the night. It was an uncomfortable journey. The cockpit was unheated, and the four prisoners were crammed in so tightly they could barely move. They did not know where they were going, but Patterson steered them east as best he could, following the stars.

At last the sun came up. By now the Black Mountains were far behind them, and, when they looked out of the window, they saw that they were flying over unfamiliar country: green fields, thickets of trees, and meandering streams. A town lay ahead, and beyond it the distant sparkle of the sea.

"Look!" cried Toni. "It's the sea! I've never seen the sea in all my life!"

"There's no snow!" marveled Sim. "I can't

believe it. Imagine it being winter—and no snow!"

They flew over the town and looked curiously down on it. There was a canal with boats, a church with a tall steeple, a town hall with a weather vane in the shape of a dragon. Most of it was a mix of ordinary houses and the gray buildings the Black Squads put up wherever they went. But a closer glance revealed that the gray buildings were in the process of being demolished, and there were other signs, too, that things were changing. In the very middle of the town stood a castle with two towers. Colorful banners snapped on its turrets, and its soft gray stonework glowed pink in the dawn light.

"Land there!" Toni pointed to an open stretch of grass adjoining the castle. Patterson pulled the lever that said DOWN, and the dragonet started descending out of the sky.

"You're going too quick!" yelled Wilcox. "Pull up! *Pull up!*"

He grabbed at the controls, and Patterson slapped back his hands. The dragonet lurched sideways in the air, and everyone screamed. Patterson gave Wilcox a shove and wrenched the joystick toward him. There was a tearing sound as the dragonet hit the turf and scraped across it. It bounced several times, came to a momentary halt, then tipped sideways. With a jarring crash, it fell on its side and was still.

Toni screamed. Sim yelled, and Wilcox kicked and struggled. "Whoa!" cried Patterson as he slid off his seat and thudded into the tangle of arms and legs. "What a landing! Anybody hurt?"

Wilcox groaned theatrically on the bottom of the pile. Patterson wriggled free his arm. He grasped the handle of the cockpit door, wrenched it down, and kicked the door open with his booted foot. A gust of air washed over his face, not frigid like the air they had left behind in the Black Mountains, but cool and clean and fresh.

Patterson stood up. For a moment he looked out across the grass to the castle, at the church steeple, towering in the distance, to the streets and houses of the town. Then he started to smile. "Well, who'd have thought it," he said softly. "My friends, welcome home. We're in Ashby Water."

chapter two

The Stolen Dragonet

Inside the Ashby Dragon House, Queen Dragon and Lily Quench were eating breakfast when they were interrupted by a tremendous crash outside.

"Goodness!" Lily jumped and dropped her sausage. "What on earth was that?"

"It sounded metallic." Queen Dragon looked up hopefully. Every week, a load of scrap metal was delivered to the dragon house for her to eat. A dragon her size took some feeding, however, and she was never averse to the odd extra snack. "Shall we go and see?"

She crawled out along the passage into the botanic garden. Lily followed her. It was still early in the morning, and the grass was cold underfoot and heavy with dew. Because it was winter, there were not many plants in the beds, but even if there'd been a forest of trees, it would have been impossible to miss the black, evil-looking object that lay crashed at an awkward angle between two flower beds. It was about the size of a car and shaped vaguely like a small dragon, with a sinuous neck and tail and scale-shaped armor plating. The red eyes still glowed, and, as Lily watched, puffs of smoke emerged from an exhaust pipe at the rear. A Plexiglas cockpit door stood open on its hinge. Lily walked up and looked cautiously inside. It was empty.

"It's a dragonet." Lily shivered. Dragonets were fiendish weapons, the work of the Black Count, who had once ruled the kingdom of Ashby. The count was dead now, and his heir, Gordon, was hiding in the past, but the Black Empire still existed and was Ashby's deadliest enemy. There was nowhere else this dragonet could have come from. And there was nothing to explain why it had been abandoned here, right in the middle of Ashby Water.

"Hmm." Queen Dragon looked at the dragonet with interest. She had eaten several during a visit to the Black Mountains and was trying to remember what they tasted like. "As I recall, they weren't half bad—whoops now, who's that?" She reared back as a blue-clad figure darted out from behind the toppled dragonet and made a run for it across the grass. Queen Dragon blinked, then quickly reached down with a claw and scooped the fleeing figure up. It screamed with terror and writhed in her scaly grip.

"Don't eat me! Don't eat me!" Lily caught a glimpse of a young blond man. "Please, please, don't eat me!"

"Eat you?" said Queen Dragon in a puzzled voice. "Why on earth would I do that?"

As she spoke, a very young woman appeared from under the dragonet. She was wearing a greatcoat several sizes too big for her, and her brown hair stuck up in spikes. In her hand she held a pointed stick that Lily recognized as a plant stake. It still had dirt on the end where it had been pulled out of the ground.

"Let him go!" she shouted. "Let him go, or I'll—I'll spike you!"

"Spike me? With *that*?" Queen Dragon looked at the stake, then at her covering armor of bright red scales. "Now that's *really* silly."

"Put him down! I mean it!" The woman waved her stake inexpertly in Queen Dragon's direction. Her voice was firmer now, and there was a determined expression on her face that showed she intended to do her best regardless of how scared she was. Queen Dragon sighed.

"I'm sure you do. Honestly, anyone would think I posed some sort of threat. All I was trying to do was stop him from running away." She looked disapprovingly at the young man. He moaned in her claw and went limp.

"I don't think he'll be going anywhere, Queen Dragon," observed Lily. "It looks like he's fainted."

"So he has," said Queen Dragon. "What a nuisance." She put the unconscious intruder down gently on the grass. The woman threw away her plant stake and fell to her knees beside him.

"He's dead!" she wailed. "You've killed him! Murderer! Brute! *Animal!*"

"Animal!" Queen Dragon bristled. *"Animal!"*

"She doesn't mean it, Queen Dragon," said Lily hastily. She crouched beside the woman and put a gentle hand on her shoulder. "Don't worry, I'm sure he'll be all right. My name is Lily Quench, and I'm a member of the Royal Council of Ashby. Who are you, and what are you doing here?"

"I'm Toni," said the woman fiercely. "This is Sim. We are—*were* slaves in the Black Mountains. We escaped from the mines in that dragonet. *Oh!*" She started, and Lily swiveled on her haunches and saw a party of people walking rapidly toward them. Leading the way was the long lanky figure of Ashby's King Lionel, wearing jeans and a bulky sweater, and Queen Evangeline, now very fat, for she was expecting a baby in about a month's time. They were accompanied by several members of the Royal Guard. When she saw the guards, Toni went pale and flung her arms protectively around Sim. His eyelids flickered, and he started to moan and wake up.

The king and queen walked right up to them. Lionel cast his eye over the dragonet, and his friendly face became stern. He turned to Lily.

"Who are these people?" Behind him, several

members of the guard started shoving at the dragonet with their brawny shoulders. It rocked briefly, then suddenly tipped back and landed on its feet. The lights in its eyes went out, and the engine died. Lionel looked grimly at Sim and Toni.

"Who sent you?"

"No one sent us," said Sim faintly. "We came ourselves."

"We're looking for help for Manuelo!" burst out Toni.

"Manuelo?" Queen Evangeline exclaimed. "You mean, you're not working for General Sark?"

"Never!" cried Toni. "I hate Sark. I would never work for him! Manuelo forever!"

"Indeed," said Lionel. As he spoke, two more guards appeared from behind the dragon house leading a third coveralled figure, a burly man with a stubbly chin. He was wearing handcuffs and one of his guards had a bleeding nose. "And who's this? Another friend of Manuelo's?"

"That's Wilcox," said Toni sullenly. "He's with us."

"Another one!" exclaimed Evangeline. "Lionel, how many of these people are there?"

"I don't know, but I plan to find out," said the king. "Guards, take these three back to the castle for questioning. Secure them in the north turret. Advise Sir Jason Pearl, my chamberlain, and report to me."

Sim and Toni went pale. "We won't tell you anything!" Toni shrilled as they were led away. "Sim and I will never betray Manuelo!" She was still shouting wildly as the guards led her into the castle and the portcullis gate came down.

Lily stood watching them go. A feeling that something was very wrong had been growing inside her, but she could not put a finger on what it was. The dragon scales on her left elbow, which normally reacted at the first sign of danger, were also tingling sluggishly. But for once, Lily could not tell what danger had set off the tingling. She knew only that the sensation had not been there when she and Queen Dragon had first found the dragonet. Troubled, for she was not used to such mixed signals, Lily turned to the king and queen.

"Well, Lily. What do you think?" asked Lionel.

Lily hesitated. "I don't think they're bad people," she said at last. "At least, Sim and Toni aren't. But I do think their being here could be dangerous for Ashby."

"I agree," said Lionel. "And I intend to find out what they're up to. Manuelo tried to steal the Treasure of Mote Ely from us, and his friends are no friends of ours. See if you can work out where the dragonet came from, Lily, and report to me in the castle in about an hour. One way or another, we're going to get to the bottom of what this Manuelo business is all about."

As soon as Lionel and Evangeline had gone, Lily climbed up the side of the dragonet and dropped into its cockpit. It did not take her long to search. There was nothing to find, except some crumbs from a sandwich under the pilot's seat and some maps of the Black Mountains which had obviously been used by the original pilots.

"They might come in handy," said Queen Dragon when Lily showed them to her. "Is there anything else?"

"Not that I can see." Lily wrinkled her nose. "It certainly smells awful in here. I'd hate to think when those miners last had a bath. Let me try and work out the controls." She slid into the pilot's seat and scrutinized a large red button marked IGNITION.

"Give it a whirl," said Queen Dragon cheerfully. "It's not going to take off by itself."

"All right." Lily jabbed her finger at the button. At once the engine coughed and buzzed into life. The control console lit up, and a lever to Lily's right glowed with a green light and began to beep.

"UP," Lily read. "And this one says DOWN." Quickly she went over the rest of the instruments. Each one was clearly labeled: ALTIMETER, SPEEDOMETER, OUTSIDE WINDSPEED. A simple joystick controlled the steering and acceleration, and there was a lever to release the wings. It all seemed extremely simple and clever, and despite herself, Lily could not help being impressed. If she had needed to, she suspected she could probably have flown the dragonet herself.

"Yoo-hoo!" called a voice. "Yoo-hoo, Lily, is that you?"

"Uh-oh," muttered Queen Dragon. "Here's trouble."

Lily killed the engine and stood up. A man and

a woman were strolling across the grass. The man was dressed as a jogger, and the woman had an unmistakable shock of dyed purple hair. Crystal Bright, the mother of Queen Evangeline, was one of the most disliked people in Ashby. She was also an attempted traitor, who had tried to hand her son-in-law's kingdom over to General Sark.

Crystal waved and blew her a kiss. "Hard at work, dear?"

"You could say that," said Lily. She never trusted Crystal, but when she was trying to be nice, there was usually extra need for concern. Meanwhile, Crystal's companion was running appreciative eyes across Queen Dragon's gleaming scales. He craned his neck to look at her head, about four stories above the ground, and whistled through his teeth.

"Before you say anything further, I am a dragon," said Queen Dragon. "Not a lizard, not a beast, and certainly *not* an animal." Her encounter with the miners clearly rankled.

"But of course you are a dragon." The man doffed his woolly beanie and bowed before her, flashing a set of very white teeth beneath his beard. "A dragon, and of royal mien. How do you do, ma'am? I am honored to meet you."

Queen Dragon relaxed a little. She was always susceptible to flattery. "I'm very well, thank you," she said. "And whom do I have the honor of addressing?"

"My name is Patterson, ma'am." The man bowed again. "I confess I am newly returned to these parts. This charming lady has been so kind as to show me the gardens."

"Very kind, I'm sure," said Queen Dragon. Crystal bared her teeth in what Lily presumed was supposed to be a smile. She and Queen Dragon had always disliked each other intensely.

"Who's that?" said Lily suddenly. "Is it a friend of yours?" A man was running toward them in an agitated fashion. He was wearing a blue coverall that looked vaguely familiar. All at once, Patterson went deathly pale.

"Best be going," he said, and, before the astonished eyes of everyone, he turned and bolted away.

"Stop, thief, stop!" the other man shouted. "Stop him! He's stolen my clothes!"

"Well, Murdo," said Dr. Angela Hartley, "it looks like you're leaving us at last."

Murdo sat on the edge of his hospital bed, a pair of metal crutches across his knees. A small duffel bag full of new clothes was on the floor at his feet. He was wearing a gray track suit and sneakers, and he kept wiggling his toes as if his sneakers felt funny on his feet. In fact, they did. In the past, where he came from, sneakers did not exist.

"I'm sure the Thwaites and Tom will look after you well," said Angela kindly. "It'll be difficult at first, but remember, if you need help, you can always find me here."

She reached out her hand for his, but Murdo ignored it. It wasn't in his nature to thank people, even ones who had saved his life. Instead, he leaned on his crutches and stood up awkwardly. That he could walk at all was a miracle, but it wouldn't have occurred to Murdo to thank Angela for this either. All he wanted to do was get away as quickly as he could.

Only a couple of months before, Murdo had

been pushed down a well. He had cracked his skull and broken both his legs, and had almost died. If he had stayed in his own time, when the accident had happened, he certainly would have. But Lily Quench and her companions had used an Eye Stone, a magical passage through time, to bring him into the future. Here, in Dr. Hartley's modern hospital in Ashby Water, he had slowly been nursed back to health.

Nobody liked Murdo. He was both violent and a bully, and there was only one person whom he truly loved: his older sister, Veronica. Veronica loved him, too. But she had been left behind in their own time and, like everyone else Murdo had known there, had been dead and buried for almost two hundred years. It was when he realized this that Murdo's distrust of his rescuers had kindled into a passionate hatred. They were all against him, even Lily and Angela. Worst of all, he knew from the way they avoided the subject that they were not going to let him go back. And if he didn't return to his own time, he would never see Veronica again.

"Come along now, Murdo." Mr. Thwaites picked up Murdo's bag. He was the head gardener of the Ashby Botanic Garden, a kindly man who had offered Murdo a home. He and his wife had already adopted Tom, another boy from the past, who had been rescued at the same time as Murdo. Tom was waiting for them now near the hospital entrance, a sniveling weakling whom Murdo had always despised. It was plain that he had slotted in perfectly to the Thwaites family and that he didn't want Murdo there at all.

They walked together down the hospital steps and stood on the footpath waiting to cross the road. The botanic garden was directly opposite. As the cars zoomed past, Tom sidled up beside Murdo.

"You broke my arm," he said in a low voice.

"Yes," said Murdo. His heart beat fast. He had never seen cars so close before. It was hard not to look terrified.

"I just wanted you to know I haven't forgotten."

"Neither have I."

Murdo stepped stiffly down off the footpath. The three of them crossed the road and went into the garden. As they passed around the side of the dragon house, they heard yells and the sounds of a struggle. Not far away, in a clear space between two flower beds, a fierce brawl was taking place between a man wearing a blue coverall and a bearded man dressed as a jogger. The first man was trying to pull off the second one's track suit, while a girl whom Murdo recognized as Lily Quench was wrestling with a purple-haired woman in a velvet coat. Queen Dragon loomed tall over everyone, flapping her wings in evident bewilderment.

"Give me back my track suit, thief!" yelled the man in coveralls. "You stole my clothes! Give them back!"

"I'll help!" yelled Tom. He and Mr. Thwaites ran straight into the fray. Murdo, who would have followed if he had not been on crutches, paused where he stood and stared not at the fighters, but at the sleek black shape behind them. The word "Manuelo" came into his head, and then he thought of Veronica. Suddenly, everything came together in his head, and he caught his breath.

Murdo edged carefully forward. The scuffle was getting nasty now. The purple-haired woman had started biting the man in coveralls with what were evidently very sharp teeth, and the man with the beard was down to his socks and a grubby pair of briefs. As quickly as his lameness would permit, Murdo skirted around the edges of the fray. No one saw him, even when he threw his crutches into the dragonet's cockpit and hauled himself painfully up its side.

There was no time to be frightened. He had nothing to lose, and, in any case, part of him still refused to believe a machine could fly. Murdo pushed the red button marked IGNITION and jumped as a loud rattle shook the machine. The rattle settled into a buzz and a foul-smelling puff of black smoke wafted across his face.

Now they *had* noticed what he was doing. Mr. Thwaites shouted and started running toward the dragonet. The dragon flapped her wings, and all the others stopped fighting and turned toward him, their faces writ large with fear and dismay. Murdo grasped the cockpit lid and clicked it into place, grabbed the lever marked UP and pulled it toward him. The dragonet lurched. Murdo's stomach turned over in terror, and then suddenly he was rising into the air. His fear turned to wild exultation. Ashby Water, with all its hateful memories of pain and imprisonment and loneliness, was disappearing behind him. He was going to find Veronica. One way or another, he was going home.

chapter three

The Dragon Howdah

Lily saw the dragonet rising into the air with Murdo at the controls. She did not waste a second, but jumped onto Queen Dragon's foreleg and ran up the jagged scales to her head. The moment Lily was in her accustomed place Queen Dragon sprang into the air. The dragonet was already a black dot on the edge of Ashby Water. It tilted dangerously, now this way, now that, and went up and down like a yo-yo. Clearly, Murdo was having trouble keeping it under control.

The dragonet buzzed over the Ashby Canal and

crossed the borders of Ashby Thicket. Black smoke poured from its exhaust as Murdo pushed down on the accelerator. The dragonet was built for speed and was frighteningly fast. Normally it would have been no match for Queen Dragon, but her right wing had recently been injured, and she was out of condition. Already, Lily could not help wondering whether they would be able to catch up.

The dragonet swooped down low, close to the trees. It clipped a protruding branch and sent a shower of leaves up into the air. Queen Dragon breathed them in and sneezed. A fireball shot out of her nose and scorched the treetops. Lily yelped.

"Watch out, Queen Dragon! We don't want to burn anything down!"

The dragonet rose high in the air again. Murdo was obviously getting the hang of what he was doing. Lily's first fear, that the dragonet would crash, slowly faded, only to be replaced by a growing concern about where Murdo was heading. As they left Ashby Thicket behind them, the dragonet veered sharply northwest. There was a red flash of fire under the dragonet's wings and a noise like dozens of firecrackers going off. A spatter of bullets sang past Lily's head, and she squeaked and dropped flat against Queen Dragon's scales.

"He's firing at us!"

"He's lucky I don't return the compliment," retorted Queen Dragon. Bullets were not much danger to her scaly hide, but the threat to Lily was real, and she immediately slowed. The dragonet fired a parting salvo. Lily banged her fist against Queen Dragon's scales in frustration.

"He's getting away!"

The dragonet scudded away over the Ashby countryside, the buzz of its engine growing slowly fainter until they could no longer hear it. Now that the pursuit had fallen behind, Murdo had stopped ducking and weaving, and had assumed a straight flight path. In the distance, beyond the borders of Ashby, Lily could see a black smudge on the horizon.

"He's heading for the Black Mountains," she said. "Why on earth is he going there?"

"I've no idea." Queen Dragon watched the dragonet disappear, its tiny speck lost against the darkness of the distant mountains. Her yellow eyes narrowed. "But I will say this, Lily. Our young friend Murdo may be taking on more than he bargained for."

"I'm sorry, Your Majesty," said Lily, when she reported to the king at Ashby Castle not long after. "We lost Murdo just beyond Ashby Thicket. Queen Dragon could have flamed him, of course, but neither of us wanted Murdo to get hurt."

"You did the right thing," said Lionel. They were sitting in the Royal Council Chamber, on opposite sides of the great mahogany table. The Royal Tea Tray had just arrived, and the king was doing the honors from a squat brown pot. "Have one of these cakes, Lily, they're very good. And don't blame yourself. We all know Murdo's never fitted in here. Even if he hadn't found that dragonet, sooner or later he would have tried to run away."

"What I can't understand," said Lily, choosing a cake and biting into it, "is why Murdo's heading for the Black Mountains. I would have expected him to go to Mote Ely Castle. After all, that's where he lived when he was in his own time. There's an Eye Stone there he could use to travel back to the past."

"My guess is that he's trying to find Gordon," said Lionel. "Don't forget, Murdo was in Gordon's army. He knows that in our time Gordon is the Black Count's heir; when he returns from the past, the Black Empire is logically where he'll go. As for the Eye Stone, to use its magic safely, Murdo would need a fresh supply of dragon's blood. Without it, the Eye Stone could take him anywhere."

Lily, who had personally traveled through several Eye Stones, acknowledged the truth of this. "Queen Dragon and I could go and search for him in the Black Mountains," she said, without much enthusiasm. Murdo had once tried to drown her in an underground dungeon; she had forgiven him, but she could not like him. "The only way to stop Gordon from coming back is to close off the Eye Stones. Now that Queen Dragon's wing's getting better, we could look for Murdo and destroy the Eye Stone at Dragon's Downfall at the same time."

"I'd like to propose a slightly larger expedition," said the king. "You see, Lily, there are bigger issues afoot here. Of course, I feel responsible for Murdo and would like to find him, but there's someone else I'd like to find, too. Someone who's sitting like a spider at the middle of a great big web of unanswered questions. Someone who may be a bigger danger to us than we realize."

"You mean Manuelo," said Lily. Her left elbow prickled ominously at the name.

Lionel nodded. "Yes. It's not so long since Manuelo tried to steal the Treasure of Mote Ely from our vaults. Now he's bobbed up again, and these miners claim they've been fighting for him. What they've told me is extraordinary, Lily. They say General Sark's losing control of the Black Mountains. Already Manuelo holds half the mines, and there's a rumor he's going to march on the Black Citadel itself. Yet nobody knows who he really is. Toni and her friends don't care, because he's freeing the miners from slavery, but what I want to know is *why* is he doing that.

I'm not convinced it's out of kindness. I'd also hate to think that army of miners might be used against Ashby."

"You're afraid Manuelo is Gordon in disguise," said Lily bluntly.

"I always have been," said Lionel. "That's why I've accepted Sim and Toni's invitation to take me to him. It's a big risk, I know, but I can't see any other way of reaching him. The Hartleys have promised to come with me as guides, and I hope you and Queen Dragon will, too. We absolutely have to find out who Manuelo is and what his intentions are."

"Of course I'll come," said Lily doubtfully. "But it will be awfully dangerous. What are you going to do when the miners find out that you're not on Manuelo's side?"

"I don't know yet," admitted Lionel. "I agree, the four miners are a bit of a worry, especially Patterson, but I can't see how I can leave any of them behind. In any case, I'm determined to go. Can you be ready to leave this afternoon, Lily, at five o'clock?"

"My bag's already packed," Lily promised. "I'll meet you at the dragon house at half-past four."

Lily left the castle and went home to the little house where she lived when in Ashby Water. It was next to the botanic garden, where the Black Count's grommet factory had once stood, and had previously belonged to her grandmother, Ursula Quench. When Lily unlocked the door, a familiar Ursula-like scent of lavender and beeswax filled her nostrils. The hall was warm from the embers of the fire she had lit that morning, and as she paused in the doorway, the grandfather clock in the stairwell chimed half-past ten and roared once, like a dragon.

Lily smiled. She had always loved the clock, with its twin dragons climbing up the casework and the carving of Matilda Quench the Drakescourge at the top. It was part of the fabric of her life, like Ursula's rose-flowered tea service, the patchwork cat in the window seat, the shabby lines of books on either side of the fireplace. But this morning Lily's sense of homecoming was quickly swamped by a huge, anxious pang at the thought of what lay ahead. Lily was used to such feelings, for she was only half a Quench, and since her very first adventure, the Cornstalk half she had inherited from her mother had shown a tendency to make her scared at inconvenient moments. Today, though, it was harder than usual for her to push her worries down. As Lily stood looking at the neatly packed satchel she always kept hanging on the hall coat stand, ready to leave at a moment's notice, she was seized by a strong desire to climb into the linen cupboard and shut the door.

Lily went into the living room and sat down by the fire. She stirred its embers, and a little flame leapt up and made her think of Queen Dragon. She was seldom far from Lily's thoughts at present, for Lily had a secret. She had been having dreams. Not ordinary dreams, but dreams so vivid they were stronger than real life. They involved Queen Dragon, and Lily knew she ought to tell her of them. But somehow she couldn't. For her dreams were of Queen Dragon's lost fiancé, King Dragon, who had been missing since the Great War of the Dragons, thousands of years before. Sometimes Lily saw King Dragon resting on a grassy cliff, and sometimes she and Queen Dragon flew together through a great natural archway into a valley where King Dragon was waiting for them. The only thing that was the same in all the dreams was the end. On the battlements of Ashby Castle Queen Dragon and Lily parted forever, Lily returning to the world of humans, while Queen Dragon passed into the realm of dragons and was gone.

Despite the sadness of the ending, whenever she awoke from one of these dreams, Lily always felt wonderfully peaceful. It was a bit like the feeling she had experienced in the Singing Wood when she had seen her grandmother Ursula, and known she was in a place where time ran differently and things had been the same since the beginning of the world. It was only later, when she dwelled on the thought of Queen Dragon leaving her, that her own fears began intruding. She had come to rely so much on her kindly presence that it was almost unthinkable to let her go. Yet Lily had always known where Queen Dragon's heart lay, and she had even promised to help her find her lost love. Remembering how readily she had made this offer, and how willingly Queen Dragon had accompanied her on so many dangerous quests of her own, Lily felt ashamed of her own selfishness, ashamed she had made a promise she was now so unwilling to keep. And yet...Lily picked up her embroidery from the sewing basket beside her chair, a half-stitched picture of Queen Dragon with her own tiny figure standing in her claw. She could not bear to think that before long this might be the only Queen Dragon she had.

She stroked the silk with her finger. "Soon," she whispered. "I'll tell her soon. But not yet."

When Lily arrived at the Ashby Dragon House, she found a strange object sitting on the grass outside. It looked like a small house with two doors, windows all around, and a complicated web of leather straps underneath.

"What's that?"

Queen Dragon looked at her glumly. "It's a dragon howdah."

"A what?"

"A dragon howdah. Apparently," Queen Dragon informed Lily, "people use howdahs when they ride on elephants. Queen Evangeline thought it would be a good idea if she adapted the design to dragons."

"Oh." Lily examined the howdah doubfully. "It looks rather uncomfortable."

"Well, it's not un*comfortable,*" Queen Dragon admitted. "Just extremely un*dignified*. Makes me look like an electric tram, or a transit bus. But don't tell the queen. She thinks it's marvelous, and I'd hate to hurt her feelings."

Lily opened a door. The effect inside was not unlike the interior of a caravan. There were padded benches around the walls, curtains on the windows, and a table in the center, fastened to the floor. The whole thing smelled of very fresh paint. A few cushions had been scattered on the benches, and there were luggage racks under the seats with a picnic basket in one of them. There were even oil lamps hanging from the ceiling. Queen Evangeline, it seemed, had thought of everything.

"How many people will it hold?"

"Ten, in a pinch," said the queen, coming up behind her. She had a long list in her hand and was checking it off. "The howdah has to be strapped to Queen Dragon's head, so as not to interfere with her wingstrokes, and that restricts the size. Queen Dragon, we're ready to strap you in now."

A troop from the Royal Guard approached the howdah, and Queen Dragon lowered her head onto the ground, a resigned yet pained expression on her face.

"Hup! Hup! Hup!" The guards lifted the howdah onto their own shoulders and started maneuvering it into position. Queen Dragon endured the process patiently, but Lily could tell from the wisp of smoke that floated from one nostril that she was getting agitated. Nor could she pretend that the howdah looked anything but extremely silly. It was painted bright blue and gold, the Ashby royal colors, and the general effect was of a bizarre Easter bonnet.

"That's brilliant!" Evangeline beamed. "Queen Dragon, it's everything I hoped for. Hop in, Lily, and we'll start passing up luggage."

Lily climbed up a rope ladder to the howdah door. It was a clever idea, but she still felt sorry for Queen Dragon. Parcels, boxes, and bags containing stores and provisions were handed up and stowed under the benches. She had just helped the guards put away the last one when the king arrived, accompanied by the four miners and Crystal. Crystal was clutching Patterson's arm and weeping loudly into a handkerchief. Patterson sighed heavily and patted her on the shoulder.

"Never mind, my love," he said. "What the king commands, must be." At this, Crystal gave a loud shriek and fainted. Immediately everyone rushed up, trying to revive her. Patterson started sneaking away.

The king stepped quickly forward. "Going somewhere?"

"Honestly, Mother," said Evangeline disgustedly. "Can't you do better than that? It's the oldest trick in the book."

Patterson shrugged. "Worth a try," he said resignedly. As he climbed into the howdah, the last travelers arrived. They were Dr. Angela Hartley and her husband, Trevor, the minister of the Ashby Church. Both were wearing bulky sweaters (Angela was a great knitter) and Mr. Hartley carried a leather flying coat and hat. Lily knew both of them were very familiar with the Black Mountains, but she also noticed shrewdly that they evened the numbers between her and

Lionel and the miners. The fact made her feel slightly better, but she still did not want to go.

The last of the luggage was lifted into the howdah and strapped down tightly, and the final farewells were made. Lily opened the window and leaned out, waving. Evangeline produced a camera from her pocket and snapped off a photo. Queen Dragon winced and hurriedly shook out her wings.

"Good luck!" shouted the queen, and blew her husband a kiss. The miners looked around nervously, and then everything started moving. The dragon howdah creaked and rocked, and everything seemed to skew around like a ship at sea. The picnic basket slipped out of the luggage rack, and Lily fell off the seat and landed on her bottom.

"I knew Evie forgot something," remarked King Lionel. "Seat belts."

Lily picked herself up. Far below in the botanic garden Evangeline and Crystal were waving good-bye. Then the dragon howdah settled into position and the first clouds streamed past and then below them. They were airborne, and Ashby Water had vanished into the mist.

chapter four

Return to the Black Mountains

Queen Dragon flew on toward the setting sun. For a little while its orange light filled the howdah, and the travelers had to draw the curtains against the glare, but it did not take long for it to drop below the mountains. Mr. Hartley lit the lamps that hung from the ceiling. Since Queen Dragon had warned them the journey was likely to be a slow one, the travelers made plans to settle down for the night.

The four miners, who had missed out on one night's sleep already, ate an enormous meal from the picnic basket and dozed off on the benches.

Lionel, Lily, and the Hartleys made plans and pored over maps Mr. Hartley had brought from his previous visits to the Black Mountains.

"According to Toni, Manuelo was in Mine II and trying to break into Mine III when they left," said Lionel in a low voice. "At that point Mine III was still held by Sark's Black Squads, though by now, of course, everything could have changed."

"Manuelo's being systematic, then," said Mr. Hartley thoughtfully. "Mine II and Mine III are on opposite sides of the same valley. Underground, their workings run very close together. It wouldn't be hard at all for determined people with the right equipment to break through from Mine II into Mine III."

"How many mines does Manuelo control?" Lily asked.

"Too many for comfort," said Lionel. "Sim and Toni seem to think it must be six or seven mines. Effectively, that means he holds about three mountains and their passes."

"That's a lot!" Lily stared at the wavy black contour lines on the map.

"It's even worse than it sounds," said Angela.

"The mines Manuelo has control of are the best and richest producers. Those mines provide the funds for General Sark to feed and equip his armies. Give Manuelo Mine III and Sark will be fighting for his life."

"Hmm," said Lionel. "The people who live in the Black Mountains have always survived by raiding and invading other countries. Let's hope the general doesn't start casting jealous eyes in Ashby's direction."

"He might," said Mr. Hartley. "But remember what happened in Ashby, Your Majesty. One or two people in the right place and time, with the right attitudes in their hearts, can accomplish amazing things."

"Then let us hope there are some amazing people in those mines," said Angela, "because I know I have never seen such suffering as I saw in that dreadful place." There were tears in her eyes as she folded up the map.

They talked on a little longer, but Lily's attention drifted. The slow rhythmic beat of Queen Dragon's wings and the swaying and creaking of the howdah made her feel as if she were being rocked to sleep. At last she lay down with her head on Angela's lap. Her thoughts became muddled and then turned into dreams: dreams where Queen Dragon was leaving, and she heard the sound of dragon wings in flight over the roof of the house. Lily dropped what she was doing and cried out, running for the door. But it was too late. Queen Dragon had gone.

"Come back, Queen Dragon!" shouted Lily. "Don't leave me!"

She fell to her knees, weeping, beside the grandfather clock. Then the clock chimed the hour and the front door swung open and she was back on the battlements of Ashby Castle with Queen Dragon before her. King Dragon was at her shoulder, his golden bulk glowing in the morning sunlight. At the sight of him Lily's anxiety faded. She stood up and lifted her hand in farewell.

For a moment the two dragons stood together, smiling at Lily. Then their wings swooped back, and as one they were gone into the morning, and the whole world was ringing with the rightness of what had happened. Her heart bursting with happiness, Lily stepped down from the battlements and—

The picture in her head started breaking up. Lily struggled to hold on to it, but voices were cutting across her happiness, and it was already slipping away. For a moment longer she lay, wrapped in the glory of what she had seen. Then a voice spoke beside her, and she reluctantly opened her eyes.

"Almost there," said a man in a blue coverall. Lily blinked, and after a moment or two, remembered his name was Wilcox.

She sat up and pushed off the blanket someone had covered her with. Queen Dragon was gliding down past a huge mountain. Its jagged cliffs and ridges were covered in fresh snow, and there was a tinge of fire as the dawn light reflected on the whiteness. The air was clear and so cold it hurt Lily's lungs to breathe. The last of her dream was gone, and already the first touch of the old fearfulness was stealing into her heart.

"It's stopped snowing." Toni peered through the window. "The blizzard must have passed over."

"There'll be another, soon enough," said Patterson gloomily. He'd somehow managed to hang on to the jogger's beanie, and it was pulled down over his ears as far as it would go. "There's always a snowstorm waiting over the next mountain around here."

Angela had been following their progress with a pair of binoculars. She checked her map, then opened a window and called out to Queen Dragon that she should land over the next ridge. Queen Dragon obediently banked to starboard. She sailed over the ridge and into a valley that cut deeply into the jagged flanks of the mountain.

"Quick!" exclaimed Angela. "Look down there." Everyone crowded around her, and the howdah creaked and leaned perilously to starboard. A small dark shape could be seen in the valley, far below them. Lily looked through the binoculars and saw that it was a dragonet, lying smashed against the snow. Everyone went very quiet.

"Murdo," said Mr. Hartley. "Oh, dear. That doesn't look very promising."

Queen Dragon soared downward in circles. She landed not far from the dragonet with a gentle *whump!* and a flurry of freshly fallen snow. Lily wrapped her head and neck with a pink knitted shawl and pulled on her greatcoat and fireproof cape. She jumped down from the howdah and landed up to her waist in a huge drift of snow.

"Ooooff!" Lily struggled to free herself. The king climbed down more carefully and helped pull her out.

"Where's all this water coming from?" Patterson wanted to know.

"It's Queen Dragon. She's melting the snow she's sitting on," explained Lily. "It's because her body's so hot."

"We could do with a few dragons in the mining camps," remarked Sim. "Hot baths would be nice."

The Hartleys were already inspecting the wrecked dragonet.

"Murdo's not here!" called Angela from the ruined cockpit. "It looks like the dragonet's run out of fuel and crashed."

"Can we tell for sure it's the same one?" asked Lionel. He and Lily walked over to the wreckage. Angela picked something up off the cockpit floor and passed it down. It was a metal crutch with the words "ASHBY HOSPITAL" written in marker pen on the handle.

"Murdo always hated these," she said. "Mind you, crutches wouldn't be much use to him on snow. I wonder where he's gone? His legs were so weak he can't have gotten far."

"If Murdo wanted to find Manuelo, he would have headed for the mines," said Lionel. "We'll have to follow him. Are there any tracks?"

"Not that I can see." Lily scouted around without success. "The snow seems to have covered up his footprints."

"Then we'll have to search for him," said Lionel. "Let's split up. Lily, you and Queen Dragon head for Dragon's Downfall. Close off the Eye Stone as we discussed, and we'll rendezvous here at nightfall. The rest of us will go looking for Murdo."

"And Manuelo," said Mr. Hartley. "It will be interesting to see which one of them we find first."

Lily and Queen Dragon waited until the search party had disappeared along the valley, then took off in the direction of Dragon's Downfall. The last time they had visited the cliffs there, they had both nearly died, and although neither mentioned the fact, the memory pressed heavily upon them. It was at Dragon's Downfall that Lily had begun to realize the fight for Ashby was not yet over. As for Queen Dragon, she had other, older tragedies to remember it by, and Lily could tell from the set of her wings as she flew how reluctant she was to go back.

On their last, dreadful visit, the Black Count had plunged to his death, and his son, Gordon, had disappeared through a nearby Eye Stone into the past. His flight had set Lily off on a series of desperate quests: first, to find Gordon himself, and then to find a way of keeping him in the past. Even now he was planning his return, as the head of an invading army that would sweep everything, including Ashby, before it. Their only hope was to destroy the Eye Stones and prevent him from returning to his own time, something Lily and Queen Dragon had discovered how to do at the cost of tremendous peril to themselves. They had flown across half the world into unimaginable places, making new friends and deadly enemies in the process. Among the enemies were the evil magicians who had helped start the Great War of the Dragons that had led to King Dragon's disappearance. It was at Dragon's Downfall that the war had taken place. It was still a stark and desolate, lonely place, and Lily could not help having mixed feelings as they approached it.

Queen Dragon landed on the cliff top, safely away from the Eye Stone's needle-shaped pillar. "I wish I could get this thing off my head," she grumbled as Lily climbed down from the howdah. "I've got an awful itch on my upper dorsals."

"Sorry, Queen Dragon." Lily rubbed her gloved hands together and walked over to the cliff edge where the Black Count had fallen the previous spring. A river flowed in the valley far below, churning whitely over jagged rocks. The cliff top did not immediately look much different, but there was an indefinable something that made the hair rise up on the back of her neck. Lily shivered, and turned to see Queen Dragon looking somberly at a rocky outcrop.

"Over there," she said. "That was where I last saw King Dragon. He told me to hide from the fighting, and then he disappeared through the Eye Stone in search of help."

"Oh, Queen Dragon." Lily took a step or two forward in sympathy. But Queen Dragon wasn't looking. Her attention was still fixed entirely on the outcrop, and her expression was slowly changing to one of puzzlement. She began sniffing delicately at the air.

"Lily. I can smell charcoal. Over there, behind the rock." She started walking around the outcrop. Lily followed her, then stopped in shock. A small green tent had been pitched in the lee of the rock. There was a burned-out campfire in front of it. Lily walked over and prodded it nervously with her foot.

"How long since this was lit?"

Queen Dragon sniffed again professionally. "I'd say, at least last night. It's hard to be sure when it's been snowing."

"All right." Lily gingerly pulled back the tent flap. As she had expected, the tent was empty, but a groundsheet was spread on the floor, and there was a neatly rolled-up sleeping bag in one corner. A cardboard box contained provisions: some bacon and sausages, handily frozen in the icy air, canned soup, and apples and oranges so hard they could have been shot from a cannon. There was also canned milk and tea in a packet. In another box were a teakettle and a camp saucepan, two bowls, two mugs, and two plates, along with cutlery. Whoever had made this campsite had every intention of coming back to it.

Lily went back out.

"It looks permanent," she reported. "There's lots of food in there, enough for two people. What I want to know is, why would anybody want to camp up here?"

"I can think of one good reason." Queen Dragon nodded grimly toward the Eye Stone. "That."

Lily's eyes widened with horror. She ran across the snow to where the Eye Stone pointed like a finger at the sky, going as close to it as she dared. Sure enough, the surrounding snow was churned over with two sets of footprints. One set belonged to a person wearing snowshoes, but the other looked to have been made by a pair of hiking boots. Lily set her foot beside one of the marks. It was bigger than her little foot, but not that much bigger. It could have been a woman's—or a boy's.

"Gordon?"

"Looks like King Lionel's guess was right all along," said Queen Dragon. "I wonder who he's been meeting?"

"I don't know. But whoever it was, they must have been here early this morning," said Lily. "There was a blizzard yesterday. Any footprints would have been completely covered over—and the campfire, too." She thought hard. "Gordon said he would come back into our time. But he always said he'd come with an army. If we're right, and the tent belongs to Gordon, what's he doing?"

"Who cares?" said Queen Dragon. "If we close this Eye Stone off now, we trap him. End of story."

"Not necessarily," said Lily. "What if Gordon *is* pretending to be Manuelo? Closing the Eye Stone off won't stop him then. Manuelo's already got an army. The miners are revolting all over the Black Mountains in his name."

"Hmm." Queen Dragon gnawed her lip with her jagged teeth. "What do you think we should do?"

"I think for the moment that Eye Stone has to stay," said Lily. "Come on, Queen Dragon. Let's get back to the valley and find the king."

chapter five

Wanted, Lily Quench

By the time King Lionel and his companions reached the end of the valley, dark clouds were massing in the sky, and the temperature had fallen several degrees. They had been walking for hours and were feeling cold and extremely discouraged. Though nobody said anything, everyone was thinking the same thing: that finding one lost boy in the middle of what was starting to look like a war was like searching for a needle in a haystack.

"My feet are sore," complained Patterson. In the haste to leave Ashby, no one had noticed he was still wearing the shoes he had stolen from the jogger. It now transpired that they were too tight for him. "I think I've got a blister."

"Serves you right for being a thief," said Toni primly.

"It didn't bother you when I was picking the lock on that prison cell."

"Please try not to fall behind," said King Lionel sharply. He waited for the stragglers to catch up and continued, "It's dangerous here, and we must stay together. Angela, can you do something for Patterson's foot?"

"I can give him some Band-Aids." Angela unshouldered her backpack and produced some strips. The party halted while she stuck them on Patterson's white, dirty, and rather smelly foot.

He wiggled his toes. "Ministering angel, you save my life."

"That blister's not too bad," said Angela dryly. "I think you'll survive."

A low angry buzz came swooping toward them around the bend in the valley. "Dragonets!" shouted Mr. Hartley, and immediately everyone ducked behind some nearby rocks. Patterson yelled and snatched at his shoe, which was still sitting out in the open; Mr. Hartley grabbed him and pulled him down out of sight. Toni wrapped her arms around her head and cowered behind them. A flight of five dragonets swept overhead in tight formation, patrolling the valley. Black specks showered down over the rocks from the machines' exhausts, and they disappeared behind a spur of rock ahead.

The king's party stood up and brushed the snow off their clothes.

"That's the biggest patrol so far," said Angela. It was the third time they had been buzzed since entering the valley. Though they had encountered nobody on the ground, there was other evidence, too, that Sark's forces were massing ahead. The snow was churned by dozens of tank tracks, moving in convoy toward the mines, and there were footprints and rubbish left by passing troops.

"It's too late to go back now," said the king. "Angela, you lead the way. Come on, everyone."

The party set off again, the four miners bickering among themselves, the king and Mr. Hartley bringing up the rear.

"It sounds like they're ganging up on Patterson," said King Lionel in a low voice. "I never realized how much the others disliked him."

"Sim and Toni obviously think that because they support Manuelo they're somehow better than someone who's just a thief," said Mr. Hartley. "I'm not sure they're right. From what we know about Manuelo, he sounds like a dangerous, unpredictable sort of character. At least Patterson is honest about what he is—and about not wanting to be here."

"I wish he wasn't," said Lionel frankly. "He's done nothing but complain ever since we left."

"It's hard to blame him for not wanting to come," said Mr. Hartley. "The one I'm curious about is actually Wilcox. He doesn't say much, but he watches the other miners like a hawk. It's as if he doesn't trust them—or he's nervous." As he spoke, Angela gave a cry and darted off into the rocks ahead of them. Lying slumped in the snow between two boulders was a human-looking shape. It was wearing what looked like a dark-colored track suit and lay very still.

Lionel stopped dead in his tracks. "I think we may have completed the first part of our quest," he said. "It looks as if Angela's just found Murdo."

Lily finished smoothing over the last of her footprints in the snow around the campsite. For the last half hour she had backtracked over every step she had made since her arrival at Dragon's Downfall, rubbing out each one with her hands until the snow forced its way into her gloves and made her fingers ache with cold. It had been hard work, but Lily and Queen Dragon had decided they simply couldn't risk the owner of the campsite coming back and finding a strange set of footprints outside his door. Even if it wasn't Gordon, it had to be someone who knew what the Eye Stones were for—and in Lily's experience, that meant trouble.

"I think that's it, Queen Dragon." Lily straightened up and rubbed her aching back. Her friend sat, not far away, in the middle of an enormous patch of melted snow. Lily knew they ought to do something about this as well, but the puddle was so huge it was impossible to work out what. Lily could only hope that there would soon be another snowfall thick enough to hide the mess.

"I'll probably start a legend about a monster,"

said Queen Dragon, looking at her tail marks. "The Abominable Snow Dragon of the Black Mountains, or something like that."

The silence of the mountains was broken by a low, malevolent buzz. Lily drew closer to Queen Dragon and looked anxiously upward. The sound deepened and grew louder, and then she saw it: a flight of dragonets skimming in V-shaped formation over the next mountain, like metallic baby dragons, belching smoke.

"What are they doing?"

"I don't know. Let's hope they don't look in our direction." Queen Dragon crouched watchfully in the snow. It was hard to tell where the dragonets were traveling, or what they were searching for, but Lily had a horrible feeling they were heading into the valley where they had left the others.

She and Queen Dragon waited until the sound had faded and the dragonets had gone. A faint drift of exhaust fumes tickled Lily's nose. Queen Dragon stood on the cliff edge and sniffed the air.

"The wind's swung around to the west," she said. "Come on, Lily. Let's get back to the others. I think the weather's about to change."

Angela gently rolled the fallen figure over and lifted back a bloodied mass of hair. Now that they were close, Lionel could see that the dark clothing was not a track suit but a Black Squad uniform. It was not Murdo but a stranger, a boy about Murdo's age or a little older, with light brown hair and fair, freckled skin. An ugly cut stood out against the pallor of his forehead. There was blood all over the snow.

Angela ripped off her glove and felt for the boy's pulse. "Too late, I'm afraid," she said sadly. A snowflake fell on her cheek, and she absently brushed it away. She pointed to the wound on his head. "He's been hit by something with a sharp edge, like a shovel. It looks to me as if the poor boy was knocked out and left here to freeze to death."

"Poor boy?" Toni bristled. "He's not a poor boy. He's the enemy!"

Angela rounded on her. "The enemy? How can you say that? His mother was probably a slave down in the mines, like you. He would have been taken away when he was born and put in the

Black Squad nurseries. I've seen those boys training in the citadel courtyard, day after day, out in the snow with their rifles. I've treated them when their fingers go black with frostbite. And you call him the *enemy*? What hope does anyone have in a system like that? What choice did he have about who he became?"

"Someone has taken his greatcoat," said Patterson quietly. "And his rifle. They usually carry their equipment in a pack on their back. And hard biscuits in their pockets, in little tins."

Mr. Hartley knelt and gently put his hand into the boy's pockets. They were empty.

"If he was ambushed by miners, they might have stolen his coat and provisions," said Sim reluctantly. "We have so little here, we tend to grab whatever we can find."

"Look," interrupted Wilcox, "I know this is all very sad, but I thought we were here to find Manuelo. From the look of that sky, there's another snowstorm coming down off the peaks. If we don't get under cover soon, we're going to freeze ourselves."

King Lionel looked up. The first snowflakes were fluttering down out of a lowering sky, and the winter's day was drawing in, sooner than anyone had expected. "What do you suggest we do?"

Wilcox pointed to a tunnel opening between two nearby rocks. "I suggest we go underground."

"Underground?" Sim looked in dismay at the entrance. "We can't go in there. That's Mine III. When we left, it was still under Sark's control."

"Some of the entrances cross over," said Wilcox. "It's Mine II."

Sim shook his head. "I'm telling you, it's Mine III."

"Some of the tunnels do come up on this side of the valley, Sim," put in Toni. "I worked in Mine II for a while. The workings run very close together."

"Do you recognize this entrance?" asked the king.

"I'm not sure," admitted Toni. "I don't know the outside very well. But once we were underground we'd soon come across a passage marker. They number the tunnels so the guards can find their way around."

"In that case, we'll chance it," said Lionel. "I

don't like the look of those clouds, or of all those tank tracks heading for the main entrance." He shouldered his backpack and led the way across the snow to the gap in the rocks. Four or five rough-hewn steps led down to a metal gate. It was dark and gloomy, and everyone turned on their flashlights. Sim went up to the gate and gave it a shake.

"It's locked."

"Allow me," said Patterson. He reached into his coverall pocket and pulled out a length of wire. As he did, a folded piece of paper fluttered to the ground.

Lionel picked it up. The paper had the pulpy feel associated with official documents from the Black Citadel that he remembered from his days as a librarian. As he unfolded it, he knew instantly what it was. Lionel stared at it, then swung up his light so the beam shone directly in Patterson's face.

"Stop right there," he said, and lifted up the paper so the others could see.

It was a wanted poster with Lily's picture on it.

The beam flickered over Patterson's face. In the gloom of the rocks it made him look like some sort of monster who had been suddenly unmasked. For a moment, the whole group stood frozen, and then automatically Sim, Toni, Wilcox, and Mr. Hartley fanned out across the steps, blocking his escape. Patterson looked from one implacable face to the next. His dark eyes glimmered with fear.

"Step away from that gate," said King Lionel in a low, even voice. "You traitor. Who are you working for?"

"Traitor?" For the first time since his escape, Patterson sounded taken aback. "I'm not a traitor!"

"Explain this, then!" Lionel shoved the Lily wanted poster under his nose. "What was that doing in your pocket?"

"I—" Patterson looked blankly at the poster and shook his head. "I—I don't know. I don't know where it came from. You have to believe me!"

"Don't believe him!" snarled Wilcox. He thrust himself forward and shook his fist in Patterson's face. "You thief! We always knew you were no good. You've brought us all into a trap!" Wilcox grabbed the collar of Patterson's coverall and threw him back hard against the gate. They grappled furiously for a few seconds, then tilted over and fell onto the floor. Sim and Lionel grabbed Patterson's arms, and Mr. Hartley and Toni seized Wilcox's. Together they managed to tear the two miners apart.

"Stop this!" ordered the king. "How dare you fight in my presence?"

"You're not my king," spat Wilcox.

"That's right," jeered Patterson. "*He* won't take orders from the king of Ashby."

"I am not ordering you as the king of Ashby," snapped Lionel. "I am ordering you as the leader of this expedition. I am responsible for everyone's safety, and I expect you to remember it." He picked up the wanted poster, which had been dropped in the struggle. "I also expect an explanation for this."

Patterson shook his head. "I don't know. No... wait! It's coming back to me. I think I found it in the guardroom on the way out, when we were escaping from the cells. They had posters all over the walls, and I put one in my pocket. You remember?" He turned eagerly to the other miners, but Sim and Toni looked doubtful.

"You mean the room where we ate the sandwiches?" said Sim at last. "Yes. I think there were posters on the wall, but I don't remember what they were."

"I was too hungry to notice," said Toni.

"Listen." Patterson started getting angry. "I'm telling the truth. What are you doing this for? You *need* me. I'm the only person in this party who can open this gate."

"Actually, I think not." Angela appeared at the top of the steps. She held up a length of chain with an elaborate-looking steel key on the end. "I found this around the dead boy's neck. I think it's a passkey. Try it and see if it works."

She tossed the key down the steps. Lionel caught it, pushed Patterson aside, and inserted it into the lock. The gate clicked and opened.

With a desperate cry, Patterson whirled around, shoved Toni aside, and ran for his life up the steps.

"Bring him back!" shouted the king. The party broke up in confusion. Sim and Mr. Hartley pounded up the stairs in pursuit of Patterson.

Toni scrambled up from where she had fallen. Before Lionel or Wilcox could stop her, she pushed open the unlocked gate and darted away down the passage on the other side.

"What's she doing?" shouted Wilcox in a fury. "Has everyone gone mad?"

"I expect she's trying to get to Manuelo," said Lionel resignedly. "Let her go. I can't see that it's going to make things worse than they are already."

"I don't agree," Wilcox began, but Lionel shook his head. Several minutes went by, and they heard the sound of footsteps coming back. It was Sim and Mr. Hartley, breathless from their run, and alone.

"We've lost him," said Mr. Hartley. "It's started to snow again, quite heavily. Patterson's disappeared into the rocks. I hope he'll be all right."

"He should have thought of that before he ran off." Lionel bit his lip in vexation. "This is a real problem. I wonder whether we should go back and find Lily and Queen Dragon. If Patterson fetches the Black Squads, he can lead them right to us."

"Not if this mine is controlled by Manuelo,"

said Angela. "Anyway, I don't think we can go back, Your Majesty. There's a blizzard starting, and in the Black Mountains they can go on for days."

"If you ask me, I think Patterson is a red herring," said Mr. Hartley, stooping. "We're exactly where we ought to be. Look at this."

He picked up a small white object and held it out to them. It was a plastic bracelet with a clip fastening and black printing on it that read ASHBY HOSPITAL: PATIENT ID 0907. Underneath it in black felt pen, a nurse had written the patient's name, MURDO.

"Murdo!" exclaimed Lionel. "Then he's here after all!" The sound of running feet was suddenly heard in the passage beyond the gate, and he looked up, half expecting to see Murdo himself hurrying toward them. Instead it was Toni. She clattered through the gate and fell to the ground, gasping for breath.

"We've made a mistake. This isn't Mine II, it's Mine III. I saw the numbers on the passage walls. This is the entrance to the wrong mine!"

chapter six

The Song of the Miners

The flight back from Dragon's Downfall took longer than Lily expected. A stiff wind had blown up, making Queen Dragon's progress slow, and though she did not complain, Lily could tell she was tiring. Then the snow came. It eddied around the windows, and the howdah was buffeted back and forth, creaking and groaning against its straps. Lily clung on grimly to her bench, green with motion sickness. Despite her many layers of clothing, she was frozen to the marrow and longing for the nightmare journey to end.

At last, Queen Dragon landed in the valley. Lily opened the starboard door. A gust of wind and snow burst through, stripping the heat out of the tiny cabin and tearing the door from Lily's hand. It flapped back and forth furiously, smashing the window behind it, and then it ripped from its hinges and flew off into the whiteness.

Lily slid down Queen Dragon's side into the snow. She staggered to her feet and stumbled back against Queen Dragon's warm and reassuring flank. She could hardly recognize the landscape as the one she had left that morning under clear blue skies. The crashed dragonet was gone, but whether it had been buried by snow or taken away, Lily had no way of knowing.

"Queen Dragon! Are you sure this is the right place?"

"Hard to say." Queen Dragon looked around anxiously. "I'm quite sure it's the same valley. But I can't promise it's the exact spot where we left the others. It's just too hard to see with this storm."

"What should we do?"

"What was that?" Queen Dragon could barely

hear. Her head was covered with snow. If it were possible for a dragon to look cold, she did now.

"We have to find shelter!" Lily shouted. "If we stay here any longer, I'll freeze."

Queen Dragon seemed to catch what she said, and nodded. "I'm going to sit behind that slag heap."

She waddled off, leaving Lily to follow as best she could. The wind repeatedly blew her over, her pink shawl was ripped from her neck and whirled away, and her fireproof cape streamed behind her like a flag flying from a pole. If it had been made of less strongly woven material, it would have been ripped to shreds.

"There's a gap in the cliffs over there, Lily." Queen Dragon pointed with her claw. Lily saw a dark opening in the side of the cliff. It was far too small for Queen Dragon, but Lily knew her situation was too desperate to be picky. She staggered toward it, her eyes and lungs burning. An iron concertina gate sealed the opening. Lily's heart sank, but when she put out her gloved hand, it squeaked and pulled back under her touch. The lock was broken.

By now the last of the light was almost gone. Lily reached for the flashlight she had put in her pocket and squeezed around the gate into the tunnel. At once the noise abated slightly, and the wind stopped. It was still terribly cold, but at least her clothes were no longer being ripped from her body and she could breathe without difficulty. Lily pushed her hair out of her eyes with a shaky hand and tried to put her clothes back to rights. The folds of her greatcoat were caked stiff with snow, and her fireproof cape hung like a dishrag from her neck. Snow had driven down her boot tops and was melting slowly into her socks.

Lily shook out her clothes and tried to empty the snow out of her boots. She was still trying to put them back on when someone grabbed her unexpectedly from behind and threw her up against the wall.

"Who are you? Who are you for?"

Lily winced and blinked. A bright light was being shone in her face, and at first she was dazzled and could not see. Then the light swung aside a little and she realized that a pale-faced woman was standing in front of her with a lantern. She was dressed in a faded blue coverall, and she looked lean, hungry, and mean.

The woman was flanked by an old man and a girl about the same age as Lily. Each wielded a raised shovel, and the girl was making unconvincing threatening noises through her teeth. The woman with the lantern held a rubber truncheon, the same weapon Zouche's Black Squads had once used to threaten the workers at the Ashby Water grommet factory. Since the woman was plainly not a soldier, Lily guessed that hers must have been stolen.

She lifted the truncheon now and thrust it into Lily's face. "Who are you?" she demanded again.

"L-Lily Quench."

"Who are you for?"

"For?" Lily did not understand. "What do you mean?"

"I mean, whose side are you on?" said the woman impatiently. "Who do you fight for?"

"I'm not on anyone's side," said Lily. "But I fight for King Lionel of Ashby."

"Ashby!" The old man immediately lowered his

shovel. The woman looked taken aback. It was clearly not an answer anyone had expected.

"Careful, John," said the woman. "It's sure to be a trick."

"It's not a trick," said Lily. "It's the truth. I do come from Ashby."

"Angela Hartley was from Ashby, Iris," said John. "Don't you remember? She was in the same slave intake as me. She set my broken leg. And she delivered Phoebe, here, and her little sister."

"Grandpa's right, Iris," put in the girl. "Dr. Hartley saved Mama's life. She used to bring us food from the citadel, behind the Black Count's back."

"Shut up!" snapped Iris. She circled around Lily. "Take off that cloak and your coat so I can search you."

Lily dropped her fireproof cape and greatcoat on the ground. Phoebe immediately snatched up the coat and put it on. Iris took Lily's sword and scabbard and frisked her to make sure she had no hidden weapons. When she had finished, Old John picked up the fireproof cape and handed it back to Lily. She put it on again gratefully, shivering with cold.

"What do we do with her now?" asked Phoebe.

"She doesn't look dangerous to me," said John. "I think we should let her go."

"The best spies are the ones you don't suspect," Iris retorted. "Who is this Lionel of Ashby, anyway? I've never heard of him. For all we know, he's General Sark's best friend."

"Well, she's certainly not a miner," said Phoebe enviously. "She's too well fed for that." Lily felt sorry for her.

"There's a chocolate bar in the pocket of that coat," she said kindly. "You can eat it if you're hungry." Phoebe put her hand into the pocket and pulled out a bar wrapped in bright red foil. She gasped with excitement and started fumbling with its wrapper.

"Phoebe, don't eat that!" ordered Iris. "It could be poisoned." She snatched the chocolate bar away and dropped it into her own pocket. Phoebe set up a wail of protest.

"You're stealing it! Manuelo said we had to share! He said we had to share everything! Give it back to me!"

"No!"

"It's mine!"

"It's not!"

"It is! Give it back to me!" Phoebe screamed and flung herself at Iris. She delved a hand into her pocket, and there was a sharp tussle. Iris hit out with her truncheon and missed, then slipped and fell over. The chocolate went flying out of Phoebe's fingers. It skidded across the darkened floor and landed at Lily's feet, but neither Phoebe nor Iris seemed to notice. For half a second, it occurred to Lily to run. She could easily get a start on them while they were fighting, and she doubted Old John would be strong enough to stop her getting away. But as quickly as the idea came, Lily knew it was no good. She could not go back out into the blizzard, and if she ran deeper into the mine she would only get lost and end up being recaptured.

"Be quiet!" she shouted. "Stop it!" She picked the chocolate bar up and waved it at them, then started unwrapping it as noisily as she could. The rustle of the foil somehow penetrated Iris and Phoebe's racket. They stopped fighting and stood up, panting. Lily broke the chocolate up and held it out to them.

"I've come to speak to Manuelo," she said loudly. "Please. Will you take me to him?"

Except for John, none of Lily's captors had ever tasted chocolate before. It helped a lot, as did the furry toffees Lily found in another pocket. Perhaps because the Black Count had been so down on sweets when he ruled Ashby, Lily had developed rather a sweet tooth since King Lionel's return; and by the time the miners agreed to take her to Manuelo's hideout, they were all sucking furiously on toffees. From the mine's entrance they went down in an elevator to a lower level, crossed several passages, and descended two flights of stairs. They were now in a rabbit warren of darkened shafts and tunnels. Even if she had been free to leave, Lily could not have found her way back to the surface, and her eyes began to ache from the unaccustomed darkness.

Everywhere she went were signs of destruction. Whole tunnels had collapsed or been destroyed, and the remaining passages were littered with broken machinery and smashed-up weapons. There were numbers on some of the tunnel walls, but most of these had been splashed with paint or hacked out of the rock. Lily guessed that someone had done their best to deface them to stop their enemies from finding their way around.

Those enemies now sat, tied up, along the tunnel walls: row after sullen row of defeated Black Squad soldiers. The prisoners had been stripped of all their equipment and, in some cases, their clothes down to their underwear. Some were hurt or unconscious, and some were so ominously still Lily feared they must be dead. Troops of miners wielding Black Squad weapons guarded them; they swaggered along the corridors in a jubilant mood, devouring what looked like army rations out of little tins, or dancing about in stolen greatcoats. A group of girls was marching up and down, arms around one another's shoulders, singing a rough sort of song that was somewhere between a hymn and a football chant. Lily tried to catch the words, but it was hard to make them out.

"What are they singing?" she asked.

Iris snorted. "Some rubbish about Manuelo.

Those kids get carried away sometimes. The way they go on, you'd think he was some sort of superhero."

"It's a good song," muttered Phoebe under her breath, and she started humming along. A little later they passed another gang, bellowing the same song. This time, Lily got the gist of what they were singing.

The hand of Manuelo
Will strike down our foes.
Manuelo's triumphant
Wherever he goes.
We'll die for Manuelo,
We'll give up our lives,
To see him victorious
We miners will strive.

Manuelo! Manuelo!
We'll die for Manuelo!
We'll follow Manuelo
Wherever he goes.

There were more verses, but Iris kept Lily moving with her truncheon in the small of her back, and she was past before she could make out the rest of the words.

The chorus followed her along the passage, distorted by echo before it finally faded into silence. They had now come to what seemed to be the deepest and darkest part of the mine. There were few miners and no prisoners to be seen. It was quiet and strangely warm. Suddenly two miners, a young woman and a man with an eye patch, came looming up out of the blackness. They appeared so noiselessly and unexpectedly that it was all Lily could do to keep from screaming.

"Password!"

Iris nervously cleared her throat. "Victory or death!"

"State your business."

"Patrol Seventeen reporting in with a new prisoner. Reckons she works for King Lionel of Ashby, name of Lily Quench. She says she wants to speak to Manuelo."

The guards conferred, and the one with the eye patch went back along the passage as silently as he had come. When he returned a few minutes later, he was frowning, as if something had not turned out as he had expected.

"Manuelo will see the prisoner now," he said. He sounded a little disapproving. "She's to go alone. Wait here."

He took Lily by the arm, not roughly, but firmly enough for Lily to realize what might happen if she did something wrong, and marched her away along the passage. Lily said nothing. For the first time since her capture she felt truly frightened. Though she and Lionel had talked about finding Manuelo, she had never expected she would have to face this meeting alone.

A little light glimmered ahead of her, then grew fainter, as if someone had deliberately dimmed it. Suddenly, Lily's guard stopped, and she saw they had reached a wooden door with a metal grille, like a prison cell. The guard opened it and pushed Lily through into a chamber on the other side. For a moment she stood, unable to see who or what was in the room. A feeling of panic rose inside her. She took a step forward and blundered into a piece of furniture. Then something gleamed in the farthest part of the room, a tiny light like a dying flashlight beam, so dim it was hardly there.

Instinctively Lily took a step toward it. Perhaps the light was not as dim as she thought, or perhaps her eyes were growing accustomed to the darkness, for she now saw that the room was furnished with a blanketed camp bed, table, and chairs. A muffled figure in a cloak was standing in the corner. As Lily approached, it turned, like a shadow swooping toward her.

"Welcome, Lily," Manuelo said. "I've been expecting you."

chapter seven

Manuelo Attacks

"Sit down, Lily," said Manuelo. "We have a great deal to talk about." He pulled out a chair and sat at the rough wooden table in the center of the room. The dim light, Lily saw, burned in an earthenware lamp in a niche on the wall behind him. It cast Manuelo's face into even more shadow than before, so that Lily could not even tell whether he was black or white. His hands were completely covered by a pair of padded, black leather gauntlets. Only his eyes gleamed brightly within the dark swathes of his cloak.

He gestured to the other chair and, reluctantly,

Lily pulled it out from the table and sat down. Part of her brain was still trying to recognize Manuelo's voice. For a moment, it had sounded vaguely familiar, but it was hard to be sure.

"What do you mean, you've been expecting me?"

"I've been expecting you ever since I visited Ashby Castle," said Manuelo. "I knew Lionel would send you eventually. It was the logical thing for him to do. You're looking for Gordon, the old count's son, of course. I'm afraid King Lionel was mistaken. You won't find him here."

"How do you know?" Something about Manuelo's manner, his mysterious insistence that he knew everything, was rubbing against Lily's nerves. And she was also annoyed she couldn't identify him. She was pretty sure now that his voice wasn't Gordon's, but it still sounded weirdly familiar. It was a strange, gruff, down-in-the-throat sort of voice, that sounded as if its owner was trying hard to disguise it. She looked Manuelo straight in the eyes. "As a matter of fact, I'm not looking for Gordon. I'm here to find a boy who ran away from the Ashby Hospital. He stole a dragonet and is missing somewhere in this valley. His name is Murdo."

"Murdo—?" The name seemed to spring to Manuelo's lips. He managed to turn it into a question, but Lily was sure that it had meant something to him. He sat very still, then, after a moment, said, "I will send my miners to look for him at once. This valley is a dangerous place: I would not like your friend to be captured by Sark's troops. Don't worry, Lily. You have nothing to be afraid of. You may find this hard to believe, but I am a better friend to Lionel of Ashby than you know."

"If you're a friend of King Lionel, why did you break into his castle?" Lily countered. "You tried to steal the Treasure of Mote Ely. Queen Evangeline caught you red-handed."

"I did it because I needed the money, of course." Manuelo seemed to have recovered his equanimity. "Revolutions are expensive, Lily. Anyway, who's to say the Treasure of Mote Ely even belongs to Ashby?"

"Finders, keepers," retorted Lily. Strictly speaking, the treasure had been found back in the past by Murdo's half-brother, Rabbit. But Rabbit had never claimed the treasure, and when Lily had returned to her own time, she and her friends had retrieved it from its hiding place. "The Castle of Mote Ely is inside Ashby's borders. Any treasure with no owner that's found in Ashby belongs to the king."

"Who says I obey Ashby's laws?" Manuelo jeered.

"If you did," said Lily with spirit, "you would never have tried to break into Ashby Castle in the first place. But let me tell you something. If you try again, I'll do everything in my power to stop you."

Suddenly Manuelo laughed. "Bravo, Lily. King Lionel's a lucky man. I only wish my own followers were as devoted to me as you are to him."

"I thought they were devoted," said Lily, surprised. "I thought they'd follow you to the death. That's what they were singing on the way down here."

"They all sing that song," said Manuelo wryly. "Some of them even believe it. But most of them just want to get out of the mines. They're happy to follow me when things are going well. But if I fail?" He shrugged. "They'd melt away like snow in summer."

"People are like that everywhere, though," said Lily. "At the end of the Seige of Ashby, when the Black Count's armies stormed Ashby Castle, there were only a hundred people left defending it. King Alwyn died on the battlements, with his sword in his hand."

"I suppose he had no choice at that point."

"He had no choice at any point," said Lily. "That's what being a king is about. I know Lionel would much rather be a librarian, with a little house full of books, and a family, and all those comfortable things everybody wants. But a king was born to put his country and his subjects before himself. Even if they hate him. Even if they kill him."

"That's a heavy responsibility," said Manuelo.

"Yes," Lily agreed. "Lots of people aren't up to it. Lionel's great-grandmother, Queen Josephine, used to drive my ancestor Amy Quench insane. She was always sending her on stupid quests to get jewels for her dresses, or gold cups for royal parties. When a dragon attacked one of the palaces, Amy was away collecting a load of antique furniture, and a lot of people were killed. Queen Josephine was one of them. Lionel's always said it served her right for being so selfish. And he's right. If Queen Josephine had been doing her job and letting Amy do hers, all those people might have lived. We none of us get to decide who we're born. But we all have a responsibility to choose who we become." She looked Manuelo squarely in the eye. "It's a ruler's job to make sure his subjects get that chance to choose."

A soft knock sounded on the wooden door.

"The miners are about to break through into Mine III, Manuelo," said a muffled voice on the other side. "They're ready to breach the passage wall on your orders."

"Excellent. We won't wait another moment." Manuelo stood up and shook his cloak folds down around his ankles. "You might like to come with us, Lily. I've already told you I am not an enemy of your king. Perhaps this is the best way for you to understand my intentions."

Lily inclined her head. She seemed to have little other choice, though she would have preferred the conversation to have continued. She followed

Manuelo out into the passage. The other guards were waiting for them, Iris still holding her rubber truncheon.

Manuelo beckoned her over. "Corporal Iris. Your unit will take care of Duchess Lily during the breakthrough. Remember, General Sark would love to get hold of her. Protect her with your lives, and do not let her out of your sight."

"You can depend on me, Manuelo," said Iris. Even in the poor light, Lily could see her flush with pleasure. Manuelo clapped her briefly on the shoulder, then strode off down the tunnel, flanked by his bodyguards.

"I've never been so close to Manuelo before," said Phoebe breathlessly. "Oh Lily, what was he like?"

Lily shrugged. "I don't know. Not what I expected."

"Come on." Iris ordered. She took Lily by the arm, and they started walking along the tunnel, Phoebe leading and Old John bringing up the rear. He hadn't said anything yet, but Lily could tell he was unhappy. At his age, she guessed, the idea of breaking through into Mine III and fighting a host of well-armed Black Squads was probably pretty scary. Or perhaps he just didn't trust Manuelo. Lily didn't herself; nor did she believe his claims to be Lionel's friend. But at least if she stayed in the thick of things, she might find out exactly what Manuelo was up to and fulfill that part of their quest.

They passed along a network of narrow tunnels and ascended in an elevator to an upper level. Most of the miners had disappeared, and only a few watchful individuals remained to guard strategic points. Iris gave out the watchword, and they were allowed to pass unharmed into a broader tunnel. It seemed to run straight through the mountain for a very long way, and long before they reached the end, Lily could feel cold fresh air blowing toward her. She pulled up the hood of her fireproof cape and wrapped its folds tightly around her, then stepped out of the end of the tunnel into an open space.

A flurry of snowflakes hit her in the face. Lily gasped, and stumbled forward, her boots catching on the uneven ground beneath the blanket of snow. They had come out into a natural cleft between the mountains, with high walls rising like a chimney shaft to the outside air. At some stage there had been a landslide, and the ground was covered with scree and broken-up rocks. Some of the rocks had been deliberately moved and placed in oblong piles, and at first Lily did not realize what they were. Then her foot caught on a loose stone, and she lost her balance.

"Careful!" Old John grabbed her arm from behind and stopped her falling. His lantern beam went flashing over the stones and in an instant Lily realized where they were. It was a graveyard. Each pile of stones was a grave, and each grave was marked with crosses made from bits of scavenged timber, painted white. Only one grave had a proper headstone. It had been carved from a piece of black rock, which had been roughly dressed and inscribed with a single name.

Lily read it without thinking. A weak feeling went rushing down her legs and she grabbed the headstone and hurriedly knelt down beside it. The name was that of the Black Count, Gordon's father. She had discovered the Black Count's grave.

The king's company was huddled by the gate between the rocks. Snow was falling, the wind was howling, and it was now pitch-dark. The situation was tense, and no one was certain what to do. They could not go out because of the blizzard, and they could not stay where they were, lest Patterson return with a Black Squad to arrest them, or worse. On the other hand, if they went into the mine, they would inevitably be found by Sark's men.

"We have to go on," yelled Wilcox, for the umpteenth time. The noise of the storm made normal conversation impossible. "If we stay here, we'll freeze."

"And if we go in, we'll get caught!" snapped the king.

"You can get caught just as easily on this side of the gate as the other, you royal moron," said Wilcox angrily.

Sim awkwardly cleared his throat. "I've just thought of something." He nodded up the steps. "That dead soldier. We've got ourselves a uniform. A disguise. If someone dresses up as a Black Squad soldier, the rest of us could pretend to be his prisoners. Yes, I know it's awful," he said as Angela opened her mouth to protest, "but so's freezing to death. He's dead, after all. We'd just need his jacket and combat pants."

"It's a way of getting into the mine." The king hesitated. "We still need to find out what Manuelo is up to."

"We've also got to find Murdo," said Mr. Hartley. "By now he could be in even worse trouble than we are."

"We'll do it then," decided Lionel. "It's certainly too cold to stay here."

He bent his head into the wind and led the way up the stairs. Out in the open it was so dark and the wind so strong they could barely make any headway. But at last they found the body where they had left it, almost covered now with freshly fallen snow. Working quickly, Sim and Mr. Hartley took off the dead soldier's boots and stripped away his outer clothes. Underneath the combat jacket and trousers he was wearing a black shirt, socks, and a set of thermal underwear.

"This uniform can't have been his originally," shouted Mr. Hartley in the king's ear. "It must be three sizes too big. This lad is scarcely old enough to have left the Boys' Squad."

Lionel nodded. "Boy soldiers in borrowed uniforms. It doesn't sound as if things are going well for General Sark, does it?"

"I'm sure it would be helpful to Ashby if we could find out." The jacket whipped in the wind as Mr. Hartley held it up. "Who's going to wear this? I'm too tall, and so's the king. It'll have to be Sim or Wilcox."

"I'll wear it," said Wilcox. He went into the shelter of some nearby rocks and hastily stripped off his miner's coveralls, revealing thick underwear and a pair of hairy muscly legs. He dragged on the soldier's padded pants, boots, and jacket. Sim and Mr. Hartley pulled Wilcox's discarded blue coveralls onto the dead soldier as best they could.

"Nobody here is going to think twice about a dead miner," said Sim. "Come on. Let's go underground."

Lily stood at the foot of the Black Count's grave, staring at his headstone. The dreadful day he had died was still vivid in her memory. She had stood on the cliff top at Dragon's Downfall with the count, Gordon, and the Hartleys. For over ten years Angela had been a prisoner of war, and now, by a miracle, she and her husband were reunited. But Angela was Gordon's foster mother, and he could not bear the thought of sharing her. In a fit of jealous rage he had tried to push her off the cliff. Instead, in the scuffle that followed, his father had plunged to his death on the razor-sharp rocks below.

Lily had thought the Black Count's body was lost forever. But the river in the valley of Dragon's Downfall was swift-flowing, and nothing lay wedged in its rocks for long. Bit by bit, bumping against boulders and eddying in rock pools, the count's body had made its final journey down the rapids to the place where the river flowed under the Dragon's Neck Mountain. The cold swift current had carried it down into the darkness of the mines, where, at last, battered and almost unrecognizable, it had been found by a party of miners in Mine II.

"How did you know it was him?" Lily asked.

Old John shrugged. "The uniform. Nobody else wore one quite like it. Sort of dark, but… grand somehow, with that iron star stitched over his breast. We didn't know exactly what had happened to him, but we'd heard about Sark's revolt, so we guessed he'd been murdered."

"He wasn't murdered," said Lily. "It was an accident. He fell over the cliff at Dragon's Downfall. He died saving Angela Hartley's life."

"Then at least he did one good deed in his black life," said Old John gravely. "I'm glad of that."

"He was certainly no friend to the miners," sniffed Iris. "If it hadn't been for you, the rest of us would have torn his body limb from limb and thrown it down the deepest shaft in the mine."

"There's no point in taking revenge on a dead body," said Old John. "Besides, the day might still come when we need to prove the count is dead. Even Manuelo agrees about that. The first thing he did when he came here was put that headstone on the grave so it wouldn't be lost."

"Come on," said Iris. "We haven't got time to waste, maundering over a grave. We've got to catch up, or we'll miss all the action." She nudged Lily across the graveyard, and a moment later they plunged into another tunnel and all was black again.

Lily walked along mechanically. It was hard to make sense of what she had just learned. In the back of her mind she saw the grassy mound in the Ashby churchyard where her grandmother, Ursula, lay buried. Lily had put a little wooden cross there to mark the spot as soon as Ursula had died, and there was now a proper headstone. But Lily had done this because she loved Ursula. She could not believe that Manuelo loved the Black Count. If Lionel had been right and Manuelo had been Gordon in disguise, it would have all made sense; but Lily was now convinced Manuelo was someone else entirely. Why, then, would he want the Black Count to be remembered?

She was still puzzling over this when they came out of the tunnel into a wider gallery. It was packed with miners, women, girls, and old men standing in ranks with their shovels and pickaxes at the ready. Three huge yellow drills had been wheeled to the front of the assembly, and the ceiling was propped up with a complicated fretwork of scaffolding. Manuelo was standing on a rock in the midst of his followers, reaching out to touch the outflung hands of those nearest to him.

"Manuelo! Manuelo! Manuelo!" the miners chanted. In the back ranks, some of the younger girls started singing "The Hand of Manuelo," bellowing the chorus over and over. Lily felt sick. She was in the presence of something horrible that she had no way of stopping. Even Iris, beside her, was grinning stupidly and shaking her truncheon, while Phoebe simply melted into the crowd of hysterical girls. Lily found herself pressed up against Old John. She glanced up and saw his face, disapproving, as if he knew exactly what was going to happen.

"My friends," shouted Manuelo. He lifted his hands, and the miners cheered and screamed until they were hoarse. "My friends! We are on the verge of a new conquest. On the other side of this wall stands our enemy. In a few moments, I shall lead us through the gap into battle. I do not know if I will live or die, but if I fall, I know my miners will be victorious. You know I hope for nothing but your freedom, and if I find it in death, so be it! The Black Squads have retreated. Now is the time to drive Sark and his men from this valley!"

Manuelo jumped down off the rock. Three

teams of tough-looking women put on eye goggles and wheeled the machines toward the wall. Lily could no longer see exactly what was happening, but she heard the drills start up and begin boring through the mine wall. Chips of rock started spewing around the mine, and a few miners jumped back as they were hit. Then suddenly there was a loud grinding sound and the first machine screamed to a halt. The operators pushed back their glasses and backed away, and the waiting miners clutched their shovels and hefted their jackhammers for the attack....

The king's company was descending deeper and deeper into the mine. So far, they had met no one, though they had heard the sound of machinery working in the distance. There was not a Black Squad soldier in sight.

"I don't understand this," muttered Sim. "The lower galleries are usually full of people. Something here is very wrong."

"Do you know where you are?" the king asked.

"Not exactly." Sim tried to sound confident, but his voice held an underlying note of anxiety. "I've never worked in these passages. But I do know they're current workings. Look at the carts, the picks and shovels. It's as if the miners have just thrown down their tools and gone."

"I can hear something up ahead," said Wilcox suddenly. "It sounds like a jackhammer. There must be someone at work there."

"Come with me. The rest of you, stay out of sight." The king and Wilcox followed the corridor around a bend. Suddenly, the tunnel gave out. A long metal ladder dropped down from the upper gallery, where they stood, into a bigger space below, a space that was full of men in black uniforms, all of them armed to the teeth. They were staring intently at a stretch of wall. It was vibrating noisily, and from somewhere beyond they could hear the whine of machinery and the rumble of breaking rock.

All at once, there was a crashing sound and a huge drill burst through the wall. It screamed to a halt, and a great shower of rock came falling down from above....

chapter eight

The Battle for Mine III

Queen Dragon was chilled to the bone. For a dragon, this was an unusual experience. As long as Queen Dragon was well fed, her own internal fires usually kept her warm, and she could hardly remember the last time she had felt so cold. But this was the Black Mountains, one of the bleakest places in the world, and she was stuck in the middle of a winter blizzard. Queen Dragon shivered and tried to push the image of her cozy dragon house out of her head. For Lily's sake, she had to endure the extremes of weather and stay where she was.

The wind howled, and the snow pelted against her scales faster than her body could melt it. Queen Dragon huddled behind the slag heap and wondered where Lily was sheltering. She had no way of telling how long she had been gone, for she could not see the stars and had lost track of the passage of time. Huge drifts of snow built up against her crimson flank, and when Queen Dragon bowed her enormous head against the wind, the howdah on her head creaked and groaned like a thing in pain.

Then she heard it. A human would have missed it, but Queen Dragon's ears were magically sharp and attuned to listen for any sound that was not the storm. It was the sound of a human moan in a male voice. Queen Dragon's dragonish eyes narrowed. Despite the darkness she could still see clearly enough to make out the miserable figure stumbling toward her through the snow. Queen Dragon recognized the blue coveralls and beanie, the familiar bearded face. With a cry of alarm she reared up behind the slag heap and the newcomer stopped in his tracks.

"Patterson! Where are the others? Where's the

king? If anything's happened to him—" Queen Dragon broke off, immediately leaping to the worst conclusion. What would she do if Lionel were dead? How would she break it to Queen Evangeline?

Patterson did not speak, but looked up at her as if she were a giant crimson mirage. His eyes were puffy slits above his cheeks, his face was blue, and his beard was encrusted with ice. He opened his mouth and closed it. Then, as if some ghost of his usual self rose up and broke through the extremity of his situation, he took a step forward and gave a stiff little bow.

"Great Queen," he said croakily. "Queen of the Dragons. I cannot express how relieved—how extraordinarily relieved—I am to see you. . . ." Patterson's voice trailed off. His eyes rolled back in his head, and he pitched face-first into the snow.

"Wake up!" squawked Queen Dragon. "You're not allowed to faint on me, I forbid it! *Wake up!* Oh, you tiresome man. Whatever am I going to do now?"

As the last drill pierced the rock wall in the cavern where the miners waited, there was an enormous rumble and an explosion of dust. The scaffold supporting the roof rattled and shook, the lights flickered, and for a moment the dust clouded everything. People screamed as they were caught by rubble or hit by invisible flying rocks from the collapsing wall, and no one seemed to know what was happening. Then the miners surged around Lily. Everything was a confusion of bobbing lanterns and unwashed bodies, people coughing and staggering, all desperate to get through the breach. The air was thick with excitement and aggression. Loud choirs of teenage girls started singing and chanting as they charged into battle, their shovels uplifted in their hands.

We'll die for Manuelo,
We'll give up our lives,
To see him victorious
We miners will strive.

With a shout, Phoebe slipped away into the crowd and was gone. Iris, too, disappeared into the general confusion. Lily shrank back against Old

John. She did not expect he would be able to do anything to protect her, but at least he seemed not to have lost every shred of common sense.

Manuelo! Manuelo!
We'll die for Manuelo!
We'll follow Manuelo
Wherever he goes.

The song's chorus echoed horribly around the cavern. Lily was not a coward, but she had seen enough of battles to realize that one way or another, many of Manuelo's followers were probably about to be killed by a large force of well-trained, heavily armed Black Squad soldiers. She felt sick to her stomach. However much the miners deserved their freedom, she could not see them winning with only shovels and jackhammers for weapons.

The sounds of fighting floated back to them from the next cavern: horrible clashes, screams, and spurts of gunfire. Lily flinched and covered her ears. She could not see Manuelo now, but the cavern they were in had almost emptied. Only she and John remained, together with some miners who had been designated as nurses for the wounded. Old John put his arm around her and they held each other tightly.

"We have to stop this!" Lily cried.

"We can't," said Old John helplessly. "All we can do is wait and see what happens next."

"Back to the others!" Lionel turned to Wilcox, but he had already fled. It was impossible to blame him. Below them, the lower gallery was flooding with miners, more than Lionel could have imagined existed. They must have outnumbered the Black Squad soldiers four or five to one, and though hardly any of them were properly armed, they fought using shovels and jackhammers with a terrifying desperation. There were, Lionel noticed, far more women and girls than men. Some of the women even had babies strapped to their backs as they swung their shovels.

The Black Squads were quickly swamped. At close quarters, with so many people milling around, it was next to impossible for them to fire their guns without hitting their own men, and they soon threw their weapons aside and started fighting with their bare hands. But it was an unequal battle. Sheer force of numbers soon pushed the Black Squads back against the cavern walls, and the miners, encouraged by how easily they were advancing, broke away in bands and started flooding down the side tunnels. Lionel turned and ran as quickly as he could along the corridor, back to where he had left the others. Miners were already overrunning the upper gallery, rushing out of side passages, and climbing up hitherto unseen ladders from the lower level. A crowd of girls came rushing toward him, almost bowling him off his feet; when the king cried out, they shrieked hysterically and shouted, "Manuelo forever!" Ahead, several more girls had caught a Black Squad soldier and stripped him to his underwear. They were tossing him violently up and down and laughing as he screamed for mercy. Suddenly Lionel glimpsed the remains of his own party, squashed up against a wall as a flood of miners rushed past.

"Wait! I'm coming!" But it was hopeless. As Lionel struggled to reach them, Sim and Toni disappeared into the crowd, their blue coveralls immediately indistinguishable from those of the other miners. Mr. Hartley vanished, too, and only Angela remained, clinging for dear life to a hydrant on the wall. Lionel reached out his hand. Their fingers touched and linked convulsively, and he started pushing his way back through the crush of bodies, dragging Angela behind him, not knowing where he was headed but simply fighting to get away.

"They're looking for the other miners!" Angela shouted. "The ones who work in this mine. The Black Squads have them shut away somewhere, and they don't know where they are. They're trying to set them free so they can join the fight."

"Where are they?"

"I've no idea. Quick, in here." Angela ducked around a corner into a narrow side tunnel. It was a dead end, and empty except for a metal cart half full of ore. A small jackhammer lay on the ground. Angela's boot scraped against it, and she picked it up.

"Look at that," she said wonderingly. "I used to use one just like this when I was a slave here, years ago. I was only in the mines for a few months, and then the count had me taken to the Black Citadel to work as his doctor. Nothing's changed. It's no wonder the miners are following Manuelo. They'd probably listen to a rabid dog if he promised them their freedom."

"Why are so many of the miners girls?" Lionel asked.

"For several reasons," said Angela. "First, because all the baby boys are taken away from their mothers when they are born and put into the Black Squad nurseries. Their sisters are left behind to grow up as slaves—provided, of course, that they survive. The miners who aren't born here tend to be prisoners of war. Most of them are women and older men. In any war, the healthy young men are the ones who fight and get killed off. Not many of them make it here in the first place."

"Three of our miners did," said Lionel thoughtfully.

"Sim is slightly deaf in one ear," said Angela. "He told me he was rejected for military service. And Patterson was a thief, sent to the mines as punishment. I'm not sure about Wilcox, though. He said he was a follower of Manuelo, but his hands look far too smooth for a miner's. I'd be curious to know what his story is."

"We'll probably never find out now," said Lionel, "but if he is a follower of Manuelo, he'll hopefully meet up with friends. What do you think we should do?"

"I think we're going to have to let Wilcox and the other miners look after themselves," said Angela. "There's nothing more we can do. Once Manuelo's followers find the other miners and let them out, this battle is really going to run out of control. We need to find Trevor and get back to Lily and Queen Dragon as quickly as possible."

"Agreed." King Lionel looked out into the main corridor. It was not so busy now, but there were still plenty of miners milling aimlessly about. Their mood had changed markedly, though, and there were no more cheers or songs. Instead, the faces were angry and anxious, and though a few women were trying to rally the rest, it seemed as if the invasion had inexplicably stalled.

Angela pushed past the king, her jackhammer hefted expertly over her shoulder. In her blue coat, she did not look so very different from the others. She spoke briefly to a young woman, who gesticulated angrily and pointed along the passage. Lionel heard the word "Manuelo" several times, then "trapped' and "ambush."

"What's happening?" he asked as Angela rejoined him.

"The miners who work in this mine are gone," she replied. "The Black Squads moved them out yesterday, and the gates that open onto the surface are all locked shut. The miners are afraid it's an ambush, and they don't know what to do."

"Where's Manuelo?" asked the king.

"That's the worst news of all," said Angela. "Manuelo appears to be missing."

As the sound of fighting faded in the adjacent cavern, Lily felt a growing sense of unease settle over her. A few shouts and skirmishes could still be heard, but the enormous clash she had expected had not happened. In her left elbow, a sluggish tingling had started up. It was not yet insistent, but the thin covering of dragonlike scales that grew there was a reliable barometer for danger. Something was obviously not right, and though Lily could not tell what it was, she knew better than to ignore the warning. She looked at Old John and saw the worried expression on his face, too.

"There's something wrong," he muttered. "What's happening in there? There should have been more of a fight than this."

A couple of miners came ambling out of the breach in the wall. One spoke to the assembled nurses, and a few minutes later half a dozen injured miners were carried out on stretchers. A few more limped after them on their own feet. One of them glanced across at Lily and John.

"They all ran away!" she called triumphantly. "So much for the Black Squads' famous courage, eh? Long live Manuelo, that's what I say!" She lifted her fist in the air.

"Long live Manuelo," Lily echoed. As she spoke, a sharp pain ran along her scaly forearm, and she gasped with shock. Old John looked at her curiously.

"What's the matter?"

"My arm..." Lily shook her head, unable to explain. "There's danger. I don't know what it is, but I think..." She swiveled where she sat and looked back along the passage where they had entered. It was dark and silent now, but she knew that somewhere along it, something was very wrong. Old John stood up. He shone his miner's lamp down the tunnel, then, unaccountably, switched it off.

"Come on, Lily. Let's go and investigate." He held out his gnarled hand, and Lily took it. The darkness of the passage quickly swallowed them. There was no light but the occasional red glow of a safety lamp, and Lily had to trust John's sense of direction, for her own was soon completely confused. The tunnel seemed to go up and down far more than it had on the way in, and once or twice she almost lost her footing on a rough piece of floor. But John stopped her from falling, and eventually, after a few minutes, Lily saw the tunnel brighten ahead.

"Is it moonlight?" she whispered. "Are we back at the cemetery?" John hushed her and squeezed her hand. They stole on a few paces farther. The tingling sensation in Lily's arm grew perceptibly stronger, and she gripped John's hand more tightly. She could hear something ahead of her—a rustling, shuffling noise. With each step it grew colder and the light grew brighter, and then they reached the end of the tunnel and found that they were, indeed, back at the cemetery. Snow was falling heavily into the well, and the graves were covered with a thick white coat that muffled the sound of footsteps and voices. For the space was no longer empty. In the unearthly whiteness, several troops of Black Squad soldiers with lanterns had quietly gathered. More were coming out of the main corridor even as they watched.

"How did they get here?" Lily whispered. "Where have they come from?"

"They must have been waiting on the surface," Old John replied. "There was scarcely an able-bodied miner left in Mine II to stop them. What I want to know is, how did they know Mine II would be empty?"

"Someone must have told them when Manuelo was planning his attack. A spy, or else a traitor." Lily laid her hand on Old John's arm. "If these Black Squads come up behind the miners, they'll cut them off. It'll be a bloodbath. We have to warn Manuelo!"

"Too late," said John grimly. Lily followed his pointing finger. At the front of the assembled troops stood a familiar masked figure. It was talking to several of the Black Squad captains. As John and Lily watched, a hand reached out from beneath a black cloak and shook the hand of the commanding officer.

Lily gasped. She could not help herself, but the sound was loud enough to be heard. John pulled her hastily down behind a pile of rubble. Manuelo stopped talking and looked across to the tunnel entrance. He started heading toward them, and, for a moment. Lily thought they were done for. But this time, the darkness was her friend. Manuelo walked on past the spot where they were hiding, and the darkness of the tunnel swallowed him up.

"Where's he going?" Lily hissed.

"I don't know," said John. "Quickly, Lily, go after him! Stop him if you can, or warn the miners. Go! You can run faster than me! *Go!*"

Lily jumped nimbly to her feet. She started running swiftly along the tunnel, one hand against the wall to keep from losing her way. A small light showed ahead of her now, as if Manuelo had switched on a lamp. Lily gained on it as unobtrusively as she could, and after a few moments, she saw the light swing inexplicably to the left. Manuelo had turned down a side tunnel, and, as she followed him around the corner, Lily tripped on something in the darkness. It seemed to be a thick bunch of wires, which snaked away out of sight into the main tunnel.

Lily looked up. Manuelo had climbed up onto a rocky platform, just above her head. His miner's lamp rested on a pile of rocks, and he was fiddling with a small box that was planted among them. A length of wire snaked away from it, the same wire Lily had tripped on and that she now recognized as a length of fuse. It must be attached somewhere to bundles of dynamite. Manuelo was going to blow up the tunnel.

"No!" screamed Lily. "Don't do it! You'll kill them all!" She jumped up and waved her arms, too late. Manuelo had already thrust down the plunger. There was a tremendous explosion, a whoosh of air and dust, and the tunnel behind her collapsed. Lily saw the ground rushing up, and all was confusion.

Lily lifted her face, coughing and spluttering. She saw Manuelo run to the edge of the rock and jump. As he fell, his cloak flew up around him. Lily had a glimpse of dark trousers and a closely fitting blue pullover, a long dark braid hanging down his back, almost to the waist. Lily registered a stab of shock, and then the fleeing figure was gone, swift, mysterious, and unmistakably female. She had discovered the secret of Manuelo's identity.

He was a girl.

chapter nine

Plot and Counterplot

In the guardroom in Mine III, a single guard sat reading a comic by lamplight. Fitz wasn't supposed to read comics when he was on duty, but tonight he was counting on nobody finding out. The mine had been evacuated yesterday, and all the prisoners had been sent to the Black Citadel. Since then, only one new inmate had come limping in, and he had spent most of his time blubbering for his sister. Fitz had jeered at him a bit, then threatened him—it was part of his job—but generally he had left him to his own devices. The guardroom had an oil heater and the cells did not; furthermore, it wasn't often that he got a chance to read *The Adventures of Count Raymond* nowadays. Since General Sark had come to power, Count Raymond had definitely gone out of fashion.

The *Count Raymond* comics were all about the original Black Count. The illustrations showed him as a great beast of a man with bulging biceps and thought bubbles full of punctuation marks. Count Raymond was given to making pronouncements such as "Die, traitor" or "I shall rip his arms off before nightfall," and his adventures generally seemed to involve killing people, torturing small animals, and conquering the world. Fitz was a big fan. He had Count Raymond socks and underpants, a Count Raymond poster in his locker back at the barracks, and (so that it didn't interfere with dress regulations) Count Raymond stickers all over the inside of his kit bag. When the last Black Count had died and the publication of Count Raymond's adventures had abruptly stopped, no one had been more annoyed than Fitz. Count Raymond's replacement, a character who was plainly supposed to remind the reader of General Sark, was in his opinion a pathetic also-ran, and the fact that the series had ended with the cliffhanger at the end of issue 157 was a source of endless frustration.

The heater purred softly, and the guardroom grew warm. Deep in the Marsh of Mote Ely, Raymond settled into the ruined castle that was his winter base camp. A mysterious youth had led him there, and Raymond did not know yet whether to trust him. Fitz, who had read this particular issue countless times, could have told him—and warned him—that this unpromising stripling, who was to become his right-hand man, would eventually betray him, but since that would have spoiled the story, he pretended not to know. In the distant galleries of Mine III, real shots were fired and people yelled, but Fitz read on, oblivious to the fighting, even when a hideous explosive rumble sent vibrations through the battered table and broke the skin on his forgotten mug of tea. It was only when a shadow fell directly over the page of his tattered back issue that he looked up, faintly aggrieved at the interruption.

A young woman in coveralls and an army greatcoat stood in front of him, her tousled head filling the gap in the row of wanted posters that lined the guardroom wall. She looked vaguely familiar, but before Fitz had a chance to do more than gape, she leaned over and ripped *Count Raymond* out of his fingers. Her companion, a young man, grabbed Fitz and held him down painfully in his chair. He, too, looked familiar, and was wearing the same blue miner's coveralls as the woman.

"Ow!" yelled Fitz. "Let go!"

"Where are the prisoners?" demanded the woman. She was trying to look fierce and almost succeeding. Fitz did his best to bluff.

"What prisoners?"

"The prisoners who were here the day before yesterday."

"No idea. Give me back my comic!"

"You mean, this?" The woman held up *Count Raymond*. Its pages creased and crinkled between her fingers. Fitz felt a flare of panic.

"Yes. Pardon me, but—that's a very rare issue. It's quite valuable—out of print—I won't be able to replace it—"

"Oh, really?" The woman kicked open the grille on the guardroom heater and held *Count Raymond* close to the oily flame. Fitz gave an agonized gasp. "In that case, you'd better tell me where the prisoners went, hadn't you?"

"Don't! Please! *Please!*"

"The prisoners!" The edge of *Count Raymond*'s cover began to smoke. Fitz screamed and burst into tears. Without so much as a thought for what his comic-book hero would do in the same circumstances, he cracked.

"They were taken away yesterday in trucks. I think they went to the citadel. There's one left; I can take you to him if you want. I promise, I'm telling you the truth! Please, please, please, give me back my comic!"

"What about the miners?" demanded the woman.

"They were taken away, too. Please, I beg you!"

"All right. Take us to this prisoner." The woman miner took *Count Raymond* away from the stove and tossed it on the floor. To his immense relief, Fitz saw that its edges were barely scorched. He allowed himself to be manhandled out of the guardroom into the passage, and he led the way down to the lower level where the prisoner was being held. As they went along his captors conversed in low voices: Fitz learned that the woman was called Toni and the man Sim. They kept talking about a king, which was strange, for there were no kings in the Black Mountains, and someone called Queen Dragon who could apparently fly. That made no sense either, until Fitz remembered the stolen dragonet that had caused so much fuss two days earlier. Suddenly he realized why these people had familiar faces. They were two of the escaped prisoners who had stolen the dragonet. Fitz's quailing heart sank even farther down into his boots. Now he was really in trouble. If his commanding officer found out what was happening, he would be lucky not to end up working in the mines himself.

They reached the cell, and Fitz cleared his throat reluctantly. "Here he is." He flicked a switch and a dim light came on. A boy sat in the corner of the cell, huddled under a blanket. His face was scratched, bruised, dirty, and swollen with crying. He was dressed in a thin gray track suit and sneakers, and was obviously perishing with cold.

Toni went up to the grille. "Who's this? He wasn't here the other day."

"He says his name's Murdo," said Fitz reluctantly. "He only came in yesterday. A patrol caught him lurking up in the valley. He was looking for Manuelo."

"Let him out," said Sim. It was the first time he had spoken, and Fitz did not miss the sense of urgency in his voice. He unlocked the door and went into the cell. Murdo cowered in his blanket and whimpered.

"Come on, you big sissy," said Fitz, feeling much better now that someone else was more scared than he was. He dragged Murdo out of the cell into the corridor and heard the unmistakable sound of a Black Squad rifle being cocked.

"Put your hands up," said a voice he recognized. Fitz's stomach turned over, a bright light shone in his eyes, and he fell to his knees in terror.

Lily sped along the darkened passages in a panic. Manuelo's explosion had sealed off the main passage. She had no idea where she was or how she was going to get out of the blocked section of mine where she found herself trapped; nor had she any idea whether Old John had been killed in the explosion. Lily could not imagine how he could have survived, and she felt helplessly angry. An old man like John was too frail to be fighting battles, and should have been allowed to die comfortably in his own bed. Tears flowed down her cheeks, and she wiped her face angrily on the corner of her fireproof cape. It did not help to know that if she had been in the tunnel with John, she, too, would have been crushed by the falling rock.

A light glimmered ahead of her at the end of the passage, and she heard the clank and whine of machinery. Panting, Lily slowed to a halt. A dimly lit elevator cage was coming down from an upper level. Lily snatched up a shovel that was leaning up against a wall and shrank back into the shadows. The cage came into view, and she saw there was one person in it, a tall man, slightly stooped but with broad shoulders. Lily raised her shovel. She growled fiercely and rushed forward, then screamed as the door opened.

A pair of kindly gray eyes looked quizzically down at her. "Really, Lily," said Mr. Hartley. "That's no way to greet an old friend."

"Thank goodness!" Lily threw her shovel on

the ground, her heart pounding with relief. She flung her arms around him, and he gave her a kiss. "I thought everybody must be dead! Where are the others? Manuelo's just tried to blow up the mine!"

"The others are quite safe," Mr. Hartley assured her. "Or at least, Angela and the king are. Our party got separated, but I found them on an upper level a little while ago. The miners told the king you were here, and we've all been looking for you. And Manuelo hasn't blown up the mine, just blocked off a tunnel. Apparently, he lured several Black Squads into a trap, at the risk of his own life. The battle for these mines is over, Lily. All the miners are going berserk with excitement. Manuelo is a tremendous hero."

"It must have been a double bluff, then." Lily quickly recounted what she had seen. "Mr. Hartley, Manuelo is a girl. I don't know who she is, but I spoke to her, and she told me she was Lionel's friend. I don't believe her—but I don't think Lionel's going to stop her, either."

"It sounds unlikely," Mr. Hartley agreed. He yanked down a handle and the elevator door rattled open. "But we've been wrong before, Lily, and sometimes it's wiser not to judge. Come on. Let's get back to the upper levels and find the king."

"What's going on here, guard?"

Fitz stood with his hands above his head. He had automatically obeyed the command to put them there, and it was a moment before he realized it had been given not to him, but to Toni and Sim. A Black Squad soldier was standing with his gun trained on them. Fitz hastily dropped his hands and saluted him.

"Good evening, sir. Just escorting these prisoners to the cells. Escapees, sir. I captured them myself."

"And the boy?"

"I was—um, just transferring him to another cell, sir. Not enough room in this one for three."

"The rest of the prisoners have been evacuated?"

"Left for the citadel yesterday morning, sir."

"Hmm. I see. Good work, guard. I'll take the prisoners with me now. Come along, you two, and you, boy. Carry on, guard."

Fitz saluted. The soldier waved his rifle, gesturing the prisoners along the corridor out of the cells. Sim and Toni walked along with their hands above their heads. They had recognized Wilcox's voice as soon as he had spoken. Although they did not know exactly what he was doing, they did not want to give his game away.

"So this is the famous Murdo," said Wilcox when they found themselves back in the main passageways. "Measly-looking specimen, isn't he? How did you find him?"

"By accident," said Sim. "We went to let out the rest of the prisoners, and he was in the cells. The others were gone. Can I take my hands off my head? My arms are getting tired."

"That was a clever idea of King Lionel's, dressing you in that uniform," said Toni.

"Yes, it was, wasn't it," said Wilcox blandly. "Where is the king, by the way?"

"We don't know," said Toni. "We were going to look for him. Now that the battle's over, it shouldn't be too hard to find him."

For the first time, Murdo piped up. "I want to go to Manuelo!"

"Now why would you want to do that, I

wonder," mused Wilcox. "Compassion? Patriotism? Adventure? I wouldn't have thought you were the type. Particularly if you can't spend a night in prison without blubbering for your mother."

"My mother's dead," said Murdo sulkily. "And you can't make me go back to Ashby. I hate it there."

"Oh, I'm not going to make you go back," said Wilcox. "Quite the opposite, in fact. Now look at this, it's our lucky day." They rounded a corner and came to a gate. A group of familiar faces turned to look at them: King Lionel, the Hartleys, and Lily. Everyone was talking and hugging one another, and Angela was unlocking the gate with her key. When she saw the new arrivals, she exclaimed in a delighted voice, "Murdo!" and reached out her arms.

Suddenly Wilcox gave Murdo a vicious shove. He sprawled against Angela's legs, and she cried out and fell backward. Wilcox cocked his gun, walked straight up to Lily, and spun her around by the shoulder.

"Drop the key," he said, "or I'll shoot my hostage where she stands."

chapter ten

The Hostage

"Who are you?" said King Lionel. His face was drained of color, but his voice was firm. "You're not a miner. Who are you working for?"

"He's a spy." Sim turned to Wilcox. "I wondered why that guard obeyed you. You're only wearing a cadet's uniform. He must have known who you really were. You're a Black Squad officer!"

"I'm a colonel in the intelligence unit," said Wilcox coldly. "I was sent to set things up with Manuelo. He was going to hand the mines over to General Sark in exchange for joint control of the Black Empire. At least, that was the agreement. I warned Sark that Manuelo would never keep his side of the bargain. I was right."

"General Sark's a fool," cried Toni. "Manuelo would never betray the miners!"

"Just as well for him that he didn't," said Wilcox. "The general had no intention of keeping his side of the bargain, either. He would have thrown that double-crossing cutworm into the deepest dungeon in the Black Citadel and let him rot forever. I was looking forward to seeing him there. The whole time I was in that cell with you two idiots, all I could think of was that Manuelo would soon be somewhere infinitely worse, and that I would have helped to put him there."

"Why were you even in the cells?" asked Lionel. "I can understand why you were dressed as a miner, but—"

"I was only supposed to be there overnight," said Wilcox. "They had to get me back to the Black Citadel without breaking my cover. A convoy was supposed to transfer the prisoners once the fighting broke out. I should have gone with it—but Manuelo started fighting a day early, and then I got caught up in the escape. I missed the convoy, but now I will make Queen Dragon take me to the citadel. I was going to use Murdo as my hostage, but Lily is a much better choice."

"If you harm one hair on Lily's head," said Lionel very quietly, "I promise you that I will come after you and deal with you personally. That is, if Queen Dragon doesn't get you first."

"Queen Dragon? That overgrown lizard?" jeered Wilcox. "Dream on, Majesty." He twisted Lily's arm and jerked her through the gate, locked it behind them with Angela's key, then gave her a vicious shove along the passage.

Lily marched along with her hands on her head, Wilcox following close behind her. He seemed to know the way, and when from time to time they came to more metal gates, he unlocked them with Angela's key. Lily had no idea where they were going, but she could tell that they were climbing up through the many levels of the mine toward the surface. Wilcox avoided the elevators, and Lily soon grew tired of climbing stairs, but she did not dare speak a word of protest. As they went up, it grew steadily colder. Without her greatcoat, Lily began to shiver, and when they reached the final gate, bigger than the rest, which opened onto the surface, she saw that the snowstorm she had sheltered from was still raging.

"Where is she?" asked Wilcox suspiciously. "Where's the dragon?"

"We landed near one of the entrances to the other mine," said Lily through chattering teeth. "I couldn't tell you where she is now."

"She's probably not that far away," said Wilcox. "This is the narrowest point of the valley. Call out to her. You're going to get her to fly us both back to the citadel."

"She'll never hear me—" Lily started to object, then saw Wilcox's expression and thought better of it. "Actually, Queen Dragon's hearing is very good. Queen Dragon! *Queen Dragon!*"

The wind tore the words from Lily's lips and whirled them away. Lily called again. Just when she was beginning to think it was a hopeless exercise, a shadow came swooping toward them. Lily was used to the speed and silence of Queen Dragon's landings, but Wilcox was taken off guard and flinched involuntarily. It was only for a split second, and Lily felt a grudging admiration for his courage. Another man would have fallen flat on his face with terror.

"Lily!" Queen Dragon greeted her. "What are you doing here? I thought you were going to shelter in the mine until the storm was over—"

"No time to talk, Queen Dragon," interrupted Lily. "The plan's changed. I want you to fly me and Wilcox here to the Black Citadel. It's urgent." She rolled her eyes frantically to show something was wrong, but Queen Dragon gave no sign of noticing. Instead, she lowered her head obediently so that Lily and Wilcox could climb into the howdah. Lily scrambled in as nimbly as she could, but any hopes she'd had of eluding Wilcox were immediately dashed. He was right behind her, and as soon as they were inside the howdah, he fastened the remaining door firmly and stood in front of the missing one on the starboard side.

"Light the lamps." Wilcox tossed a box of matches onto the central table. Lily struck one and lit the oil lanterns, her fingers stiff and clumsy with the cold.

"Now stand over there."

"Please...can I put a coat on?" Lily gestured

to her backpack, which was stowed under one of the benches with a pile of folded blankets. It contained another coat, lighter than the one she had given Phoebe, but still better than the woolen jacket and fireproof cape she was wearing. But Wilcox obviously did not care whether she was cold or warm. He pushed Lily up against one of the posts that supported the howdah roof and began tying her up with a length of cord. Suddenly the howdah lurched, and Wilcox swore. Lily gave a little cry of shock. For a moment, as the pile of blankets shifted in takeoff, she had distinctly seen a bearded face beneath the bench at the end of the howdah, a grimy finger pressed against its lips to silence her. It was Patterson.

"What's that dragon trying to do, kill us?" Wilcox stamped over to the front window. The snow was so heavy it was hard to see out. Queen Dragon was climbing steadily, but the wind was strong, and as they rose above the protection of the valley, the howdah began to sway and creak even more alarmingly than on Lily's previous journey. It seemed to be listing to port, as if something heavy was pulling it down on that side. Suddenly the port door rattled, and she saw the handle move. Lily's eyes widened. Wilcox looked up at just the wrong moment and spun around, just as Lionel smashed the glass in the door with his fist and grabbed the handle.

"Lionel! Watch out!" Lily yelled, unable to do anything else. The king was struggling with the doorknob, his right hand bleeding from a cut. The latch was clipped firmly in place, and his bloodied fingers were slipping on the metal. Wilcox grabbed his rifle and fired, but the howdah was shaking so much the shot went into the ceiling. Suddenly, the door opened, and Lionel scrambled inside. He threw himself at Wilcox, and there was a wild struggle for the gun. But Lionel, though young and fit, was not a fighter. A second shot rang out, smashing one of the oil lamps, and then Wilcox grabbed the rifle by its barrel and swiped at Lionel with it. He slipped and fell backward. Lily heard a hoarse cry, the howdah door flew open, and Lionel pitched out.

Lily screamed. Later on, she thought that nothing in her whole life could equal the awfulness of that moment. At first it was hard to believe what she had actually seen, and then a thousand thoughts came following in an instant—Lionel, as she had first known him, sitting in his dusty library in Ashby Castle; Ashby itself, without a king again; and, worst of all, Queen Evangeline and the little unborn baby who would never know its father. Lily yelled and screamed in sheer anguish. She kicked the post and yanked uselessly at her bonds until the skin on her wrists burned so painfully she had to stop. Dimly she heard Wilcox shouting at her to shut up, but it was impossible to halt her hysterics.

Great swirling gusts of wind and snow howled through into the interior of the howdah. Tears poured down Lily's cheek and started to freeze there. She saw Wilcox at the howdah door, leaning out into the darkness as if he were trying to shut it, and then she realized he was kicking it as it swung unevenly back and forth on its hinges. A human hand and a mop of curly hair were just visible through the broken window. King Lionel had one arm thrust through the window and the other wrapped around the edge of the door; his long legs flailed in the wind, and every time the door swung toward the safety of the howdah, Wilcox kicked it savagely back.

"Queen Dragon!" shouted Lily. "Land! Land!"

"Land before I tell you, lizard," shouted Wilcox, "and I toss your young friend Lily straight out the door!" The words went flying into the storm, and Queen Dragon kept flying steadily onward. She was still steering for the Black Citadel, making poor headway with her weakened wing, and there was no way of telling whether she had heard or not. Lily glanced at the pile of blankets where Patterson was hiding, then across at Wilcox. He had stopped kicking and was leaning dangerously out of the howdah toward the flapping door, trying to catch it as it swung toward him. Each time he tried to grab it, it swung backward out of his reach. Lily could see him getting angrier and angrier.

"Come here, *Majesty*." Wilcox's fingers brushed the door and almost caught it; it swung away again, just in time, and Lily caught a glimpse of Lionel's grim and frightened face. If Wilcox got hold of the door, he would slam it shut and break the king's arm: there would no hope for Lionel then, or Lily either. Again the door swung in. This time, Wilcox caught it and gave a cry of triumph.

"Patterson!" shouted Lily. *"Do something!"*

Wilcox spun around at the sound of her voice. The door flew out of his hand, and, with a roar that was half fright, half bluff, Patterson flung off the blankets and threw himself forward, head lowered. He cannoned into Wilcox's stomach and the spy fell backward against the doorframe and lost his footing. Lily did not even hear him scream as he fell. But as Wilcox slipped through the gap, the howdah door swung in again. His full weight crashed against it, and as he disappeared into the snowy void, Lionel, too, lost his grip and vanished.

"Lionel!" Lily screamed. She could not believe they had come so close to saving the king, only to lose him at this final instant. Then in reply she heard a faint, a very faint cry above the storm. Patterson knelt in the doorway, looking down.

"He's caught on the wing!"

"Cut me loose! There's a bread knife in that picnic basket. Hurry up, hurry up!"

Patterson grabbed the basket and fumbled with its straps, showering its contents over the floor. Plates smashed; knives and forks rattled; and apples from Lily's orchard on Skansey went rolling underfoot and disappeared out the door. Patterson finally found the knife and started sawing at Lily's bonds. It seemed to take forever. Wilcox had secured her tightly, and the knife was rather blunt.

"Hold on, Your Majesty!" Lily shouted. "Hold on!" The last bit of rope broke free, and she ran to the door. Immediately Lily saw that it was not as bad as she had feared. The strong headwind, and the impetus of the swinging door had thrown Lionel backward until he had hit the leading edge of Queen Dragon's wing. It had given him something to grab onto, and he had further managed to hook his arm around the huge clawlike talon that protruded from the first wing joint. But with every wingstroke he bounced and flapped up and down, and the drag of the wind over Queen Dragon's wing was so tremendous, and the cold so bitter, that Lily knew it was only a matter of minutes before the king succumbed and fell.

Lily leaned out of the howdah and shouted to Queen Dragon. Her ears were little holes in the top of her head, topped by rather goofy-looking tufts of skin and scales: they were exceptionally keen, but the headwind was impossibly strong and she could not hear. After a moment or two Lily gave up and turned to Patterson.

"I'm going to go down to him," she shouted. "Pass me that rope."

"What rope?" Patterson picked up the severed cord Lily had been tied with. Lily shoved him aside and started ransacking under the benches. Luckily Queen Evangeline was an efficient packer. Lily found another rope and tied it around her chest, taking care to leave a long loose end. She looped this around her shoulders, then lashed the other end to the central post.

"You'll have to let me down," she said. Patterson nodded and went back to the doorway. Lily stood beside him, shivering like a swimmer on a cold morning. She sat down and dangled her legs into space, then slid off the edge with a single jerky bump.

At once the wind hit and buffeted her about. Lily screwed up her face and tried to ignore the snow. Patterson started letting out the rope. Down she jerked, bit by bit, spinning around like a spider in a hurricane. The farther she dropped, the more out of control Lily felt. She tried to concentrate on Lionel below her, whose position was so much worse than her own, but it was hard to ignore her own precariousness and the deadly cold. Queen Dragon's wing was swooping rhythmically back and forth, and the forward stroke brought Lionel almost directly underneath her. Lily dropped down a few more lengths of rope and found herself suddenly almost at the king's level. Queen Dragon's wing swooped toward her like the boom on a sailing boat. The rope jerked down, she hit the bone with a jarring thud, and then suddenly the great leathery wing was rising and falling beneath her like billows on the sea.

"Your Majesty!" Lily saw Lionel not far from where she was lying sprawled on Queen Dragon's wing membrane. She started inching toward him, rolling and lurching on her stomach. The king's face was white and exhausted from the effort of holding on, but when he saw Lily, he tried to smile.

"Saving my life again, Lily?"

"Don't talk, Your Majesty," Lily cautioned him. She took the long, loose end of the rope from around her waist and bent over the bony edge of the wing. Looping it under Lionel's shoulders was more difficult than she expected. The wind was so strong she was almost blown clean away, and it was hard to get the end around his body without disturbing his precarious grip on Queen Dragon. But at last Lily managed to get it around him and secure it.

"Lily," said Lionel, "stop. This isn't going to work." He put his hand on the knot and pulled it undone before Lily could stop him. The long tail of rope flew loose and went flapping in the wind. Lily tried to grab it.

"What are you doing?"

"We can't both climb up this rope. And one man can't possibly pull up two of us. We're too heavy." Lionel looked up at the dimly lit howdah, far above them; they could just see Patterson, standing anxiously in the doorway. "You have to go back. I'm your king, I'm ordering you to do this."

"No!" Lily could not tell where the courage that seized her at that moment came from, but she knew without a doubt what she had to do. Lionel was far more important than she was. He was in danger only because he had tried to rescue her, and it was far more important that he should survive this adventure than she. He was her king, and she was his official Quencher. It was her job

to serve him and Ashby in whatever way she could. Swiftly, Lily untied the rope from under her own arms. This time it ran through her fingers as if it had a life of its own: in a moment she had looped it around the king and tied it off again.

"No, Lily!"

"Yes! You have to go, Your Majesty!" Lily leaned forward and shoved Lionel in the chest as hard as she could. He yelled and slipped away from Queen Dragon's wing, swinging out dangerously into space. Lily heard him shouting at her, then dimly saw him starting to go up the rope. She closed her eyes in relief and tried to concentrate on holding on.

Without the rope to support her, it was much harder. It was so cold and the wind was so strong Lily knew it was only a matter of time before she let go and fell. In her mind's eye it seemed to Lily that she saw her grandmother, Ursula, as she had last seen her in the Singing Wood. In that instant it seemed to her that it would not be so bad to die: she would see Ursula again, and her parents, and nobody and nothing would ever separate them again. She would be safe.... Lily looked up and saw that the king had reached the howdah. The rope was swooping toward her; they had tied a kettle onto the end to weight it, and were swinging it back and forth. Through frost-rimmed eyelids, Lily saw it coming. She tightened her grip with her left arm and reached up a hand. But her reflexes were dulled by cold and exhaustion, and she had misjudged her ability to keep holding on. Lily's left arm gave way. She lurched sideways; there was a jarring crash, and she began to fall. All around her was cold and darkness, and she knew no more.

chapter eleven

Lily's Vision

Lily sat on a sward of green grass at the top of a cliff. She looked out across the land below—the dark woods and forests intercut with the lighter green of fields and plains, the purple mountains with their snowy crests in the distance. A light breeze ruffled the grass and lifted her hair. The sun shone and she could smell the scent of flowers on the warm air, like lilies and hyacinths, and the moon roses that grew on the Island of Skellig Lir.

"You've traveled a long way to come here," said her companion. It was the first time King Dragon had spoken. His voice was rich, deep, and musical, like the slow ringing of a bell. The sweetness of the sound seemed to go on forever, dying out upon the clear air, but when Lily looked up she saw that his golden eyes were troubled. "What I don't understand, Lily, is why you are so afraid. You know what you have to do, yet you hang back. Can it be that you have lost heart?"

Lily dropped her gaze. "I don't know," she said. "I don't know what I want anymore. I started off being a Quench because I thought that was what I was born to do. Now I'm not sure any longer. I'm so tired, King Dragon. I never thought it would be easy, but it gets harder and harder every time I have to go adventuring. I'm afraid of things changing. I'm afraid of losing Queen Dragon. Sometimes, my enemy seems so strong, I think I'm never going to win."

"Only you can decide where your own future lies," said King Dragon. "However, I can tell you truly, Lily, that giving up the fight will never stop the attack or cause your enemy to turn away from you. Remember that the worst part of the battle is always just before the end, when we are tired and half despairing, and it seems there is no end in sight. There is no shame in becoming weary, or wanting to let go, but it is at this time, above all others, that we must stand firm. Never forget what you were born to, Lily, and do not let yourself be distracted. There is a plan, and your choices, if they are made honestly and truly, will become a part of that. Do you really believe that if you give up, what you love will be taken from you?"

"No," said Lily forlornly. "I suppose I don't. But sometimes it's so hard to believe that everything will come out right."

"That is the secret of faith," said King Dragon. "To believe when everything seems hopeless. To take that first step into what looks like nothing, and trust it with your life. It's a lesson I learned at Dragon's Downfall, where so many dragons died. I saw so much evil there, and afterward, that I almost gave up hope. Yet now my friends and I have a country of our own in the Vale of Eydelen, the last and biggest of the great secret places of the world. That is where you must bring Queen Dragon, Lily. You have to tell her about the visions. You have to let her go."

Lily was silent. "How do I find the way?" she asked at last.

"You cannot travel to Eydelen by ordinary means," King Dragon replied. "Like the Library of Skellig Lir and the Singing Wood, it has its own magic, that keeps it the way it was when the world was new. But the magic that holds Eydelen safe from the outside world is far stronger than the other two places; you cannot go there by chance or design, but only if you are meant to. Go to the Island of Skansey. Sit with Queen Dragon on Merryweather Hill, as you are sitting here with me now. Have faith in your heart and trust that the door will be opened to those who are meant to come."

He rose up on his haunches, and Lily scrambled to her feet. Suddenly it seemed to her that in the far distance she could see the red roofs of Ashby Water, and the royal pennons snapping on the castle turrets. Lily caught her breath. A small red fleck had launched itself from the battlements and was flying toward them. Then the world turned suddenly around and Queen Dragon had taken her place at King Dragon's side on the cliff at the edge of the world, and Lily was standing alone on the battlements of Ashby Castle in her silver armor.

"Remember," said King Dragon, "that in the end, all will be new again." His voice rang out across the farthest reaches of the world. Then he and Queen Dragon were gone into the morning and the sun was rising over the sparkling sea.

Lily blinked and opened her eyes.

The first thing she realized was that it was morning. Wintry sunlight shone through the window of the dragon howdah: she was inside, lying on a pile of blankets, with more blankets piled on top of her. Every muscle in her body ached with pain, but she was warm, in a way she had never thought to be again.

"That's better," said a voice Lily recognized. She screwed her eyes up and turned her head. A man in a leather flying jacket was sitting beside her makeshift bed, drinking a cup of tea from a thermos.

"You've been dreaming," said Mr. Hartley. "A

dream that was not a dream, but a message. I can see it in your face."

"What happened?" asked Lily. "I was falling. . . ." Her voice trailed off as she began remembering and her eyes filled with tears.

"Queen Dragon landed," said Mr. Hartley gently. "I don't know how she knew what was happening, but she did. You didn't fall far at all, and you landed in new soft snow. The king and Patterson brought you back inside, and Queen Dragon flew you back here to the safety of the valley. You saved King Lionel's life, Lily. And he saved yours in return.

"I won't ask what you dreamed," Mr. Hartley went on. "Some things are private. But it might help you to remember, Lily, that when we give something up, something else always comes into our lives to replace it. When your grandmother died, Queen Dragon came to fill that space in your life. Not to replace her, but to help and protect you. And you mustn't be afraid. Remember that a prophecy is a gift of comfort and encouragement, and that nothing is written in stone. We're not slaves, Lily. We shape the future through our own choices." A noise started up below, and they heard Murdo's voice shouting angrily, arguing with Angela and Lionel. Mr. Hartley sighed. "For good, or ill."

Lily struggled under the blankets. She managed to sit up just enough to see out of the window. Murdo was standing with his back against a rock, his arms gesticulating wildly in an oversize greatcoat.

"I won't go back!" he was shouting. "I won't! You can't tell me what to do! You kidnapped me from Mote Ely. You'll put me in prison and never let me go!"

"Of course we won't put you in prison," Lionel answered. "Don't be ridiculous, Murdo. You can't stay here, it's dangerous."

"I want to fight. I want to join Manuelo's army. Let me go!"

"It's so strange, this fixation he has with Manuelo," murmured Mr. Hartley. "I wonder what's behind it."

Lily shook her head wearily. She couldn't understand Murdo's intentions, and just now, she didn't really care. All she knew was that it was Queen Dragon who had taught her how to be a Quench. Now she must let her go, to be a dragon among dragons, the creature she was created to be.

"My head hurts," said Lily in a woebegone voice. She closed her eyes, but not in time to stop the hot tears seeping out from beneath her lids.

chapter twelve

Patterson's Curse

Manuelo had vanished. In the dark of night, at the height of the victory celebrations in Mine III, he had slipped away, leaving the miners to take charge of things themselves. It was Manuelo's way to do this, Sim and Toni explained. Manuelo worked to free a mine, then moved on and started fighting somewhere else.

"We'll see him again, soon enough," Sim said cheerfully. "He's got lots of work to do yet."

"That's what I'm afraid of," said Lionel as the miners said their farewells and walked away. "I don't play cards much, but I don't think any of us yet know what hand Manuelo is trying to play. It's true that, whoever she is, she *is* helping free the miners. But on the other hand, we still don't understand what her connection is with Gordon. I wish there was a way of keeping watch on things."

"As to that, Angela and I may be able to help you, Your Majesty," said Mr. Hartley. "We've talked things over and we've decided to stay here a little while with the miners. There's so much to do, so many people to help. We can keep an eye out for Manuelo and let you know if she reappears. We know about the Eye Stone at Dragon's Downfall, so it shouldn't be too hard. And we can look after Murdo, too. He's obviously determined not to return to Ashby, and while you could force him to go with you, I don't think it would be the answer. His leg is getting better all the time, and before long he'd be sure to run away again."

"Would Murdo agree to stay with you?" Lionel asked.

"I think so," said Mr. Hartley confidently. "He's missed Manuelo, you see, and if he's to find her, he needs some way of staying in the Black

Mountains. I'm not saying it's going to be easy for us, but Angela is very patient, and they seem to have reached some sort of truce."

"Do it, then," decided the king. "I must say, though, that it's a job I don't envy you."

Mr. Hartley's lips twitched. "Look at it this way, Your Majesty. We get Murdo; you get Patterson. I'd call that a fair exchange."

"Believe me," said the king with feeling, "it's not a fair exchange at all."

He climbed into the howdah, where Lily and Patterson were sitting together awaiting takeoff. Considering the crowd that had set out from Ashby, the howdah now seemed almost empty, especially as most of their supplies had been given to the miners. Lily, who was feeling better after a rest, was wrapped in a blanket, munching an apple. Patterson had made himself at home, and was eating a large sandwich, a slab of fruitcake, and two bananas as he drank a cup of coffee.

"Ah, this is the life," he said expansively as the king entered. "Good food, pleasant company, a little lady waiting for me back home at the castle in Ashby…"

Lionel blanched and sat down hard on a bench. "Home? My castle? You're not serious?"

"A neat house on one of the nearer royal estates would suit us equally well," Patterson conceded. "Plus a town house for shopping and socializing. I don't think Crystal cares much for the country, but I'm sure we can split our time between the two. I've always fancied myself as a country gentleman."

"Hold on!" said Lionel. "You only met Crystal two days ago. Are you telling me you're planning on setting up *house* with her?"

"Patterson says he used to know Crystal very well," Lily remarked. "They were separated by the war, like the Hartleys."

"My acquaintance with Crystal goes back many years," said Patterson with dignity. "We were, er, parted at the time of the Seige of Ashby, when I was mistakenly taken to the Black Mountains in a prison transport. I flatter myself that my beloved was pleased to see me again, but I admit there are some bridges to rebuild. My presence in the years before my departure was unfortunately intermittent."

"Heaven help me," said Lionel faintly. "Is the queen aware of this?"

"I don't think young Evangeline recognized me," Patterson explained. "In her current condition I didn't want to shock her. However, I'm looking forward to renewing our acquaintance."

"Fine," said Lionel, in an even fainter voice. "Well, Patterson. If I'm to be cursed with your presence, I suppose we'd better get moving. Queen Dragon! Home to Ashby!"

Queen Dragon lifted her wings in acknowledgment and took off. Lily leaned her forehead against the glass and stared down at the valley. It didn't look much different from the way it had on their arrival, but things had changed, were changing everywhere, it seemed, and would continue to do so for the foreseeable future. For the Black Empire, this moment was a hinge in history, a time when doors were opened or closed, and everything turned around for good or ill. It was hard to tell yet exactly how things might work out, but as she watched the Black Mountains disappear behind them, their snow-covered slopes glittering in the morning sunlight, Lily fervently hoped she would never see them again.

She slept for most of the journey and only woke when Queen Dragon started going down over Ashby late in the afternoon. The patchwork landscape of wintry fields and forests had never looked so welcome. Lily stood watching the miniature cars on threadlike roads, the tiny houses with plumes of smoke rising up from invisible chimney pots. There was no snow anywhere, and Lily felt an incredible surge of gladness. She had never felt so grateful to be alive.

"It's not a bad place, is it, Lily?" said Lionel in a low voice. "Sometimes there's nothing like coming home to make you appreciate what you have." He squeezed her hand, and they stood together at the window as Queen Dragon spiraled down over the town and landed in the courtyard of Ashby Castle. Stiff and weary from the long journey, the royal party climbed down out of the howdah. A troop of Royal Guards came up and started to unstrap the contraption from Queen Dragon's head.

"Phew. Am I glad to get rid of that thing," she said, eyeing it with disfavor as it was set down on the courtyard cobbles. "No offense to the queen, Your Majesty, but it's really not me. Too bad it's been so badly damaged."

"We'll adapt it as a potting shed for the botanic garden, Queen Dragon," said Lionel, picking up the hint. "I promise, you won't have to wear it again." A window flung open in one of the walls, and he looked up. A woman with disheveled purple hair leaned out, glaring down at him in disfavor.

"So you're back, are you? Fine husband you are. That's what men are like. Disappear over the hill at the first sign of trouble—"

"Trouble?" Lionel exclaimed. "What's happened?"

"Nothing's happened. Not yet at any rate, and no thanks to you."

"Crystal, what are you talking about? Where's Evangeline?"

"In labor," said Crystal triumphantly. "Suffering most horribly. Crying out because her husband isn't there and she's all alone."

Lionel went pale. "But the baby isn't due for another month!"

"And of course, they arrive to timetables," jeered Crystal. "Just as well my girl's mother was here to look after her. Fretting, she was. Crying for her husband, Lionel the Absent, Lionel the Unreliable, Lionel the—"

With a loud cry, Lionel dashed across the castle courtyard and disappeared inside. Disappointed to have lost her audience, Crystal sniffed and withdrew, closing the window with a sharp click.

"There's a real woman," said Patterson, admiringly. "Like a tigress with her cub. All fire and spirit, and what an eye! It fairly blazes through you whenever she looks at you. They don't make them like that anymore."

Queen Dragon made a choking noise. She and Lily exchanged glances, but it was obvious that Patterson was deadly serious.

"Personally, I think one Crystal is quite enough to cope with," said Lily as he loped off to the door.

"He's certainly smitten with her," said Queen Dragon. "You know, Lily, I've a horrible feeling that Queen Evangeline might be about to get a nasty shock."

"I only hope Patterson can afford Crystal's clothes," said Lily. "Did you see what she was wearing?" The Royal Grandmother-in-Waiting had been dressed in purple velvet with an ermine collar. She was not, strictly speaking, entitled to either, but neither the king nor queen had the energy to point this out to her.

"I'm sure he'll find the money somewhere."

"Putting it like that makes me feel even worse." Lily looked up at the window where Crystal had disappeared. It was tightly shut against the winter air, but somewhere inside the Royal Baby was about to be born, the prince or princess who would be heir to the throne of Ashby. Lily felt a little surge of excitement. Evangeline and Lionel had promised she could be the baby's godmother, and as the king's official Quencher, she would be responsible for its protection.

"I hope the queen's all right," she said. "Do you think Crystal was telling the truth about her fretting and suffering?"

"Queen Evangeline has never fretted in her life," said Queen Dragon. "As for suffering, I'm sure she'll be fine now that the king's there. Of course, it will take a little while before anything happens. Babies never come in a hurry, even human ones. Baby dragons, of course, are even worse. Not that I'm ever likely to get a chance to lay an egg." She sighed, and Lily realized the moment had come.

"Queen Dragon," she said hesitantly, "I have to tell you something important, about King Dragon. I've been having these dreams." She paused. "It's hard to talk about them. I don't really understand them. But I keep seeing King Dragon, and last night, after I fell from the howdah, he spoke to me. He said he and his companions had fled to a country of the dragons, far beyond the reaches of the world, and that they were safe there. He said it's called the Vale of Eydelen, and it's like the Singing Wood and the Library of Skellig Lir: one of the great and secret places of the world."

Queen Dragon took this in. "Did he tell you anything else?"

"Yes." Lily drew a deep breath. "King Dragon said I was to take you there. That the time had come for you to join him. I knew it already, I'd seen it over and over, but I didn't want to tell you because I was scared. You see, I was afraid I would never see you again, and I didn't want to give you up. It was selfish of me. I'm sorry."

"The problem with humans," said Queen Dragon, "is that compared to dragons, they live such a little time. In our terms, it's not much more than an eyeblink. I think, Lily, that having waited so long to find King Dragon, I can spare you as many eyeblinks as you need. There'll always be enough left for King Dragon. Will you come with me to Eydelen? Will you show me the way?"

Lily blinked back her tears and nodded. As she did, she heard the sound of a newborn baby crying from the castle window above.

"Yes, Queen Dragon," she said. "I will."